FOOLS' GOLD

DOLORES HITCHENS

FOOLS' GOLD

WITH A FOREWORD BY
DUANE SWIERCZYNSKI

LIBRARY OF AMERICA

Published in the United States by Library of America.
Visit our website at www.loa.org.

Fools' Gold was published by Doubleday & Company, Inc. in Garden
City, New York, on March 20, 1958, as a selection of the Crime
Club. An English edition was published the same year by T.V.
Boardman as part of the American Bloodhound Mystery series.
The text printed here is that of the first American edition.

Distributed to the trade in the United States by Penguin Random House Inc.
and in Canada by Penguin Random House Canada Ltd.

Cover design by Donna G. Brown

Library of Congress Control Number: 2019952175
ISBN 978-1-59853-634-8

1 3 5 7 9 10 8 6 4 2

Printed in the United States of America

CONTENTS

FOREWORD

Early in the pilot episode of *Better Call Saul*, bottom-
feeding attorney Jimmy McGill (Bob Odenkirk) is stuck
defending three young men charged with a truly heinous
crime. "Oh to be nineteen again!" he bellows to the jury.
"Ladies and gentlemen, do you remember nineteen? Me
personally? If I were to be held accountable for some of the
stupid decisions I made when I was nineteen, *oh boy wow*
. . . Which brings us to these three." He points at the
defense table. "These three knuckleheads—and I'm sorry,
boys, that's what you are—they did a dumb thing."

Now I don't know what Dolores Hitchens's family life
was like. But one thing is certain: Hitchens knew nineteen-
year-olds could be complete knuckleheads, and could be
counted on to do dumb things. Take Skip and Eddie, the
young protagonists of *Fools' Gold*, Hitchens' 1958 caper-
gone-way-way-w*rong* thriller. Bitter that life has handed
him a raw deal, Skip comes up with a plot to steal a fat
stack of cash from a high-rolling boarding house guest in
Pasadena. Skip's lifelong pal (and self-described "follower")
Eddie thinks this plot has more than a few cracks in it—but
doesn't want to disappoint Skip, who's already spending
the cash in his imagination. The caper hinges on Karen

Miller, a shy orphan girl who lives in the same boarding house with Mrs. Havermann, the widow owner who has raised her since she was ten. Karen, who's enrolled in a secretarial course, is flattered by the attention from Skip and would do pretty much anything to make him happy.

A punk kid and his two clueless worshippers, planning on a big score with no real idea of who they're robbing, already seems like a recipe for disaster. But Skip's dumbest move is telling his uncle Willy—a fiftyish ex-con who immediately sees the heist as a way out of his dead-end caretaking job. Willy, in turn, enlists the aid of an old criminal pro who soon takes charge and makes Skip wish he'd never opened his mouth.

Suddenly—and this is the genius of Hitchens's novel—you can see this going wrong in a *million* different ways. Hitchens so brilliantly establishes this hierarchy of crime that after a while, you start rooting for the knuckleheads. Skip, at worst, is guilty of trying to claw his way out of a life that seems predestined, inescapable. Sure, nineteen-year-olds can be fools. But grown-ups who take advantage of them? Man, they should know better.

In the late 1950s, drug store racks were full of juvenile delinquent pulp stories by writers like Vin Packer (the hardboiled pseudonym of novelist Marijane Meaker), Evan Hunter, and Hal Ellson. And at first, that's what I thought Hitchens was writing—a story of luckless Pasadena street kids running afoul of the law. But with the introduction of Uncle Willy and his gang, Hitchens hits the accelerator and t-bones this juvie pulp tale into the side of a late-50s model hardboiled crime caper—the kind of rough stuff

Peter Rabe and Lionel White were writing for Gold Medal Books. I don't think such a hybrid existed before *Fools' Gold* —heists were supposed to be serious adult business. Kids, meanwhile, were supposed to be getting into street rumbles, greasing their hair, and rolling cigarette packs up in their sleeves.

Today we see this fusion all over the YA bookshelves, with kids thrust into dire situations that would make those hardboiled writers of the 1950s blush. Hitchens's 1958 novel, as it turns out, is both of its time and way ahead of it. If her originality hasn't been acknowledged, it's only because those coming after failed to see her skid marks on the road.

– Duane Swierczynski

FOOLS' GOLD

CHAPTER ONE

The first time they drove by the house Eddie was so scared he ducked his head down. Skip laughed at him. Above the rattling of the motor, Skip jeered, "What's the matter with you? Afraid the old woman's got X-ray eyes or something? She's a mind reader, maybe? She's looking out now and spotting us? You nuts?" What he really meant, as Eddie knew, was that Eddie was chicken.

Now that they were past the house, headed downhill past empty lots, Eddie cast a glance back. "Hell, it's such a doggone big place, that's all. Important-looking." And in this hour of near twilight, in his opinion, kind of spooky and ominous.

"The bigger they come the harder they fall," Skip pronounced. He was peering ahead to the corner where the side street entered the main boulevard from Pasadena. Suddenly he chucked Eddie in the ribs. "Hey, there's the chick now!" His tone had taken on a certain confidential excitement.

A girl of around seventeen sat on the bench at the bus stop. She had a couple of books in her lap, one open between her hands, and her head was bent over it, the book slanted so that its pages caught the last thin light from the sky. Her hair was short and curly, a soft lustrous brown. "Look at that. A dish," Skip was saying. As they went by Eddie gave her a single nervous glance and Skip an all-out stare, but she didn't look up. She wore a plain blue coat that looked old for her, white sandals, and a small white handbag hung from her wrist. Her lashes and little winglike brows were dark against the creamy color of her skin.

"She's on her way to night school now," Skip explained. "Taking a secretarial course. The old lady tried to goose her into nursing school, but she wouldn't bite. You want to meet her tonight? I could introduce you when typing class is out. Be in the hall."

"Maybe one of us ought to kind of lay low," Eddie said. "I mean—" He paused to watch what Skip was doing with the car. Skip had waited for a lull in the traffic on the boulevard, then cut sharply into a U-turn. "Hey, for the lova Pete!"

"Just going back for another look. We've got to have that layout down pat."

"Oh, Lord." Eddie hunkered down into the seat, trying to squirm out of sight of the bench. "You want her to know we've been out *here*?"

"Why not? It's a free country." Skip often pretended to be dense like this.

"Look, afterwards, when the thing happens, won't they begin to ask about strangers hanging around, other people in the neighborhood—"

"Oh, relax, for Chrissakes." Skip swung the car jauntily close to the bench on which the girl sat, then whistled his wolf call. She lifted her face at that, staring at the car; but Eddie sensed that she hadn't recognized Skip. She wore a confused, foggy expression, as if her mind were on the book or as if her eyes, tired from reading, had trouble adjusting to the distance.

The old car puffed and rumbled as it started back up the grade. Skip nursed it with gas from the choke. Eddie said, "She didn't seem to know you."

"Getting dark," Skip said. "Anyhow, we'll meet her tonight at school."

He had already dismissed Karen Miller from his mind, Eddie saw, and was again fascinated by the house. The roof made a tall, turreted line against the darkening sky. It was an aloof and aristocratic old house, settled in amid dusty cedars and deodars, surrounded by almost a square block of lawns and shrubs. A mansion, Eddie thought, and the idea of fooling around it and the old woman who owned it made prickles of icy bumps crawl on his arms.

Suddenly a couple of lights went on inside, one upstairs and one down. "Doggone!" Skip muttered. "You see that? Both at once? Somebody's there with her. I'll find out from Karen tonight who it is."

"Maybe a maid." Eddie needed to do something with his hands, so he took cigarettes and a pack of matches from his jacket pocket and lit a smoke.

Skip shook his head. "She doesn't keep a servant. Too cheap. She makes the chick help her and together they do it all, a hell of a job from what Karen tells me. A regular moperoo."

"A place that big . . . must be a hundred rooms—"

5

"Nah. All she has is a gardener. He comes by the day, three times a week. Old guy, deaf as a post. Lives miles from here."

"Well, then, this relative of hers—"

Skip's teeth gleamed as he smiled. He was small and wiry, a reddish blond with pale, stony eyes, and when he smiled he looked like a fox. "Yeah, it must be him, the guy from Las Vegas." They were past the house now. Looking back at it through the masking branches of trees, Eddie caught a cold, faint twinkle of light like a star's, and this somehow seemed a warning, making the place more dangerous, more impregnable than ever. He choked over words he couldn't get out.

The car picked up speed as the street leveled out. Beyond the Havermann place the street skirted vacant hilly acres rising to foothills, then descended again to another through boulevard, this one cross-town from Los Angeles, the route they'd taken to get here. Neon signs and street lamps were beginning to flare against the dusk. "Well, what do you say?" Skip asked. "Want a hamburger and coffee before we go on?"

"Sure," Eddie said, trying to sound easy. His hands were cold and his fingers kept wanting to twitch; he felt a repeated need to swallow. He hoped that Skip didn't notice his nervousness, and at the same time he envied Skip's cool manner. This was something to keep you bug-eyed.

They parked near a diner and went in. It was fairly full, but they found a couple of stools near the end. When the waitress had come, taken the order and gone again, Skip began to toy with a pencil on a paper napkin. He muttered to Eddie, "I'll bet it's at least fifty grand." He wrote it out on the napkin: $50,000.00, and Eddie broke into a sweat. They were right in the open, under lights, next to other people. He grabbed the napkin and shoved it in his pocket and Skip laughed.

"What's the matter, Eddie?"

"Well, that just wasn't smart."

"Who says?"

"I do." But Eddie didn't back it up with a glance at Skip; he fiddled with the coin receiver for the juke box, reading the array of record titles, finally dropping in a dime for a tune.

"You got a complaint? You want to run this show?"

"It's still your show," Eddie said stiffly.

Skip stared for another moment and then his mood underwent one of its quick causeless changes. He stuffed the pencil into his coat pocket and slumped on the stool, bracing his head with his hand. "Oh, what the hell." He began to watch an old man working behind the counter, cleaning off the dirty dishes into a big tin tray. The man was about sixty, going to fat, had watery eyes and almost no hair, wore a white tee shirt and a white duck apron. His big arms were pocked with scars and a network of broken veins. "See him? You know what? In a few years that's you and me, Eddie old boy. Restaurant swampers. Or dishwashers. If we're lucky. If we aren't lucky we'll be hobos, freezing in rags in a culvert."

Eddie felt cornered. "Ah, don't start singing the blues for Chrissakes."

But Skip slumped lower, his eyes dull. "Figure it out. I'm

twenty-two. You're almost as old. Who're we trying to fool, going to night school, me taking typing and bookkeeping and you studying metalwork. Who's going to hire us when we finish?"

Eddie looked at him. "We could get a break."

"Who from? Some personnel manager? Some cluck too dumb to want to know what we've been doing up to now?"

Eddie shifted his position, began to fish for another dime to drop into the record player. But Skip grabbed his wrist and held it, his finger digging into his flesh. "They give you a form to fill in, see? Every year for the past five years—" With his free hand Skip sketched five imaginary lines on the counter. His lips were pulled off his teeth in a fierce, foxy grin. "Where were you last year, friend? And the year before that? Weren't you in some kind of little trouble? Would you care to give us your former address? Wasn't it out in the country and weren't you sort of working for the state?"

Skip released Eddie's hand suddenly and Eddie sat huddled, wondering who had been watching.

After a minute in a low tone Eddie said, "Look, Skip, I've told you I didn't—"

"You mean they took those two years for nothing?"

"Yes."

"That's kind of expensive nothing. Don't you think you might have some change coming?" The waitress came and put down the food and the coffee, and there was silence while they dug out the money to pay her. "Now look. Afterwards, when we're swamping dirty crockery, we can't say we never had a chance. We had a big one. We had four cherries and a bell going bong-bong-bong and everybody screaming jackpot. We just pushed it away, that's all."

"Who's pushing it away? I'm not," Eddie said humbly.

"You're not?"

They began to eat. Eddie wondered why Skip had the recurring urge to test and torment him. He ate and thought. Under the uneasiness he knew that Skip was right; there were freakish circumstances here which wouldn't be apt to happen again. How often did you run into a girl like Karen, an odd ball, trusting Skip and telling him all that stuff about the old woman and the guy from Las Vegas and the money? In some ways Karen must be a dope, because what did she know about Skip? If she had known the truth, she wouldn't have told Skip a word about anything bigger than a nickel.

Skip chewed slowly and then he said, "What we ought to do now is to go back to the house and scout around. It'll be dark. With lights on inside we might see something."

Eddie looked at him. Skip was all right again, friendly, sure of himself. "What about classes?"

"So we're fifteen minutes late." Skip shrugged.

Eddie didn't argue because he wouldn't admit even to himself the squeamish dismay in his own vitals. He had to measure up and quit being a drag on Skip. He and Skip had been friends for years, ever since grammar school, with Skip the leader and organizer and Eddie the follower. Even the separations, while one or the other served time in reformatories and jails, hadn't broken the pattern. "What do you think you'll see? The money?" he asked finally.

They went out to the car again. Skip said, "I've got to

make sure it's on the up-and-up and Karen isn't just handing me a line. I want to see the old woman and the inside of the house, and check what Karen told me. If I see the relative counting his dough, all the better."

Eddie sensed that Skip, in spite of what he said about Karen, was pretty sure of her. Skip had never had any trouble with women lying to him. Something in his face and manner discouraged it.

They drove back the way they had come. The last of the twilight had faded and the street lamps had a yellow brightness against the night. In the block next to the Havermann property a thin grove of young eucalyptus trees straggled down from the hilly rising almost to the curb. Here and there were a few wild and neglected lantana thickets almost as high as a man's head. Eddie parked, got out, looked around. He nodded toward the hills. "Up there. Get it?"

Eddie could make out only the line of hills against the sky, the thicket dark among the trees. "What do you mean?"

"High ground. We go on up there and circle around, we can look *down*. Down into the house." Skip shuffled his shoes. "Anything looks interesting, we'll creep in close."

He started off with Eddie following in his tracks. Dead leaves crackled underfoot and occasionally out of the dark the lantana brushed them with a thorny prickle. When they came to a clear spot Eddie paused and looked back and was surprised at how far they'd climbed above the road. The lights of Pasadena across the Arroyo Seco made a great glow to the east and south. To the right, far away, downtown L.A. lit up the horizon.

"Come on," Skip muttered. He circled east toward the upper end of the Havermann place. There was lawn here, glimmers of light through the thick old trees. "Well, let's try a little closer."

There was a sudden loud crashing and bounding through the shrubs and Eddie turned hot with fright. He knew at once what it must be and that Karen hadn't said a word about a dog. Skip was cursing, and then the dog jumped on him out of the dark and Skip thrashed to the ground. There was a lot of racket and Eddie stood frozen, expecting someone to follow, a light to shine on them, a gun pointed, anything. Instead the dog leaped off Skip and bounded around playfully, letting out little yelps. He wanted Skip to chase him.

Skip got up, still cursing, and brushed at his clothes. There was enough light for him and Eddie to see the dog, still leaping around and wagging his tail. "Hell," Skip said, "the damn dog didn't even bark."

"Let's go back," Eddie said suddenly.

"No, look, this is important. Karen never said a word about a dog, and I kind of hinted, too. She's holding out on me. Who does she think she is?" Under his breath he cursed the girl fiercely. "The thing is, the important thing, he's no good for a watchdog." Skip squatted and whistled softly, and the big collie came over and tried to lick his face. The dog made whining sounds and Skip patted his head.

"You don't know what he'll do next," Eddie argued. "I'll bet he's used to people hiking along up here, kids playing hooky or hunting jackrabbits. If we try to go near the house, he'll raise hell."

"Well, let's test him." Skip jumped to his feet and strode off downhill through the trees toward the lights of the house. Eddie stood rooted in the dark. The dog whined a couple of times, circling Eddie as if asking a question about what to do next, then suddenly sat down on his haunches. Eddie moved into a still darker spot, then clucked to the dog; and the collie ran to him, frisking.

"Hey, boy. Nice boy." Eddie rubbed the dog's warm silky head, feeling the hard bones of the collie's skull under the fine fur. He liked dogs generally, most especially big golden dogs with a friendly way.

Skip whistled a summons, an eerie killdeer kind of noise, but Eddie hung back, telling himself he and Skip would be better off if he stayed to keep the dog from the house. He didn't move until Skip returned, which must have been more than ten minutes later. Skip was walking lightly, confidently, hissing the killdeer cry between his teeth. He came up to Eddie, and Eddie sensed the grin.

Skip patted the dog. "The mutt likes us."

"He's a good dog."

Skip said, "I was right down there, real close, looking in the windows. Chrissakes it's big, but it's old–old furniture and high ceilings and regular granny shelves full of knickknacks. I didn't see the old lady. There's a man inside, though. He's in a room, must be a library, looking at something on a desk. I thought maybe account books, but I couldn't be sure." Skip cuffed the dog playfully, and the dog growled and pretended to chew his hand. "The guy from Vegas. He's brought more dough."

"That's a crazy place to keep money!" Eddie blurted.

"You trying to knock this thing?" Skip cried in sudden anger.

"No, of course not."

"I got a good look at the guy," Skip boasted, "real good. I'd know him anywhere. You know what I'm going to do? Before we pull this, that is? I'm going to hitchhike to Vegas and look him up."

Eddie felt his heart lurch against his ribs. "That'd be crazy!"

"Oh, I'm not going to charge in and let on I'm itching for his green stuff. What this'll be—making *sure*. Karen *thinks* he's big in Nevada, has a chunk of one of the clubs on the Strip, but she could be wrong. He could be tinhorn, full of wind, maybe even making a play for the chick. One thing more, is he really old lady Havermann's ex-son-in-law? I'll need to check on it."

"He'll have you thrown out," Eddie said.

"You think I'm dumb enough to speak to him, let him get a look at me?" Skip was outraged, on the verge of violence. "The thing is, if he's who Karen thinks he is, and he's coming here every few weeks, staying overnight, why not, if not to stash some winnings?"

"And why should Karen tell you about it?" Eddie cried from his own uncertainty.

"Because." Skip leaned toward him in the dark beneath the trees. "She's mine any time I want her. Just any time, anywhere, anyhow. Want me to prove it?"

"What do you mean?"

"We'll come back here when classes are out, I'll show you. Right here on the ground under these trees."

"Ah, can it."

"No, I'm serious."

They started to walk west, then downhill out of the trees. They had forgotten the dog, and he rushed by them suddenly, scattering leaves and dirt, and Eddie stumbled with fright. Skip whirled to look back, as if someone might have sent the dog after them: but there was only the bank of towering evergreens and the glimmer from the house.

The dog jumped around, wanting to play, but Skip ignored him.

Finally they started off again. Skip didn't say anything until they got to the car. The dog frisked off home, and Skip faced the street light and said, "If anything goes wrong on this thing, someone's going to get hurt. Bad hurt." His tone was sharp and mean.

Eddie thought, Skip's thinking about Karen. But he couldn't be sure. Skip might be thinking about him, too. It was right at that moment, stepping into the car, that Eddie realized how utterly intent Skip was on getting the money.

CHAPTER TWO

Karen Miller laid her coat across the back of the chair and looked with a touch of shyness around the room. A few students were already at their typewriters, one or two pecking desultorily at the keys, but most were still in the hall, smoking a last cigarette or lingering to finish a conversation. Karen sat down, adjusted her skirt across her knees. Her motions were deft and graceful. She put out her hands, settling her fingers on the keys of the typewriter. She ticked off a few imaginary phrases.

A buzzer sounded in the hall. There was a bustle of entry, chairs scraping, a last whisper of talk. The teacher, a tall thin man with a storklike gait, came in from the hall and smiled at the assembled class. He laid a couple of books on the desk. "Good evening, students."

The chorus answered as usual, "Good evening, Mr. Pryde."

Karen opened the exercise book on the desk beside the machine, and the memory of a whole series of nights like this, Mr. Pryde and his greeting, the waiting, hopeful, or indifferent ones around her, ticked off in her mind. The faces, the figures were familiar, and Karen thought of them as friends, though in some way she was not able to comprehend she seemed unable to make the opening overtures which might lead to actual acquaintance. It was part shyness but mostly a lack of practice in social give-and-take. She felt awkward in the presence of strangers. It seemed to Karen a sort of miracle that Skip had sought her out and forced her to talk to him.

She knew that Skip must be in his place behind her now. A feeling of warm awareness stole through her; she could almost feel his gaze on her. She wanted to glance back at him, afraid at the same time that this glance would betray all that she felt.

Mr. Pryde left his desk and stalked over to the old phonograph in the corner. He wound the old machine. "Time for an exercise in rhythm. You ain't got a thing, you know—" He paused for effect. "–if you ain't got that swing."

Titters answered the sally, not because of any humor in it, but because poor old Mr. Pryde had worn the remark to death. Karen felt a surge of sympathy for him. Mr. Pryde glanced at his watch. "Page twenty-two. Keep in time to the music. Now. *Dum dum de dum.*" A Sousa march, hoarse and brassy, roared from the machine. Karen began to type rapidly.

When the exercise was finished she took a quick glance behind her and was surprised to find Skip's place vacant. He didn't come in until the first period was almost over. He crowded close to Karen as the class poured out into the hall for the break. "Hiya."

She looked at him shyly, pink color coming into her face. "How are you?"

"Really want to know?" He made it sound as if he kept a dangerous secret, teasing her.

"Oh, tell me." They were in the hall now, strolling away from the others. She noted a certain real excitement in Skip's manner. "You must have had a good reason to miss the rhythm exercise."

He caught her elbow and took her through the door, out upon the terrace which overlooked the grounds. Lights bloomed across the campus lawns; a sprinkler sent a shower of silver over the dark shrubbery. "I feel like cutting class–period. Never coming back." With his fist he chucked up her chin, put his mouth on hers, pressed hard. Finally she drew away, gasping. "What do you mean?"

"Ah, I'm disgusted, I'm not getting anywhere." He took out a cigarette and snapped flame to it from a match, all with an elaborate air of anger.

"Oh no, Skip! You mustn't get discouraged!"

He leaned on the railing, smoking moodily. Karen stood close, as if her nearness might soothe him. "Is anything the matter? More than usual?"

"Does it have to be more than usual? Isn't the regular grind enough?"

"You're bored, Skip? Is that it?"

"Aren't you, babe?"

"No. Mrs. Havermann wants me to learn something to make a living at. She thought nursing, but I couldn't stand that. I was sick a couple of years ago, I had to have my appendix out, and I saw how those nurses worked and what they had to do. I know I'd never be a success at it. I'm not patient enough, kind enough. Why, a woman in our ward used to—" She broke off suddenly.

Skip was interested. "Used to what?"

"Oh, it wasn't a nice thing, the thing she did."

"Well, what was it?" When Karen remained abashedly silent he said, "For Chrissakes, what do you think I am? A baby? The woman wet the bed, I bet."

Karen looked embarrassedly back at the door. "Well, it was something like that, only worse. She'd use the bedpan, and then when the nurse came to take it she'd make it spill. Over and over. They must have known she did it on purpose. You could see she got a kick out of it. But those nurses just cleaned and cleaned—and I'd have blown my stack."

"So now you're taking typing," Skip put in.

"It's not exciting, but it's something I can do," Karen said.

Skip turned to her and grinned. "You know what I'd have done? I'd have taken the nursing course like Mrs. Havermann wanted. And then I'd have looked around for some rich old geezer to nurse, some old bachelor or widower loaded with dough, not too bright, and I'd have married him."

Karen was disgusted. "Some sick old man? Oh, heavens!"

"And then, being a nurse, I'd have helped him get sicker and sicker until finally he croaked and I had the dough for myself."

The thought shocked her. "That's an awful thing to say."

He moved closer and put a hand behind her head and pushed her mouth against his own. All of Skip's kisses had an experimental quality about them, as though the act of embracing contained some novelty he couldn't get used to. "Now I've made you mad."

"Well, I'm getting over it." She kissed him in return, solemnly, and as if humbly offering a gift. The buzzer sounded; he yanked her back.

"I don't think I'm going in there."

"Why not? You're doing as well as anybody. Don't quit just because tonight you're bored and disgusted," Karen begged. "They'll give your place in class to someone else, and then you'll have to start all over again next semester, just like a beginner."

"I don't know—" He seemed to hesitate. "What about afterwards?"

"You asked before; I told you how Mrs. Havermann gets nervous if I'm not there on time. She doesn't like being alone."

"Yeah, yeah. She's crazy about you."

"No, she's not. I'm not her child. It's because of her own feelings."

"Suppose there was a meeting after class, you had to stay for it?"

"There never is."

"She knows there never is?"

"Oh, Skip, I don't want to worry her!"

He nodded indifferently. "Sure. I see exactly how it is. Go on inside then. I'll see you around sometime."

She hesitated in the doorway, her expression harried and anxious. "You make it seem as if I'm letting you down."

He shrugged, turned to lean on the railing, lit a fresh cigarette, and expelled smoke into the dark. The stony eyes looked past her as he glanced into the hall. "They're all inside. You'd better hurry."

She rushed back to him headlong. "What would we do? I couldn't take time to eat, or go dancing, or anything like that."

He laughed shortly in surprise. "Who the hell said anything like that?"

"Well, then . . ." She was confused.

"I'll drive out somewhere close to the house, a lonesome spot, we'll sit in the car for a while."

She couldn't help coloring a little. "I'm not supposed to do anything like that."

"Like that? Or like this?" He threw away the cigarette, put both hands against her waist, backed her against the wall. He kissed her. "We'll leave a little early, give us plenty of leeway." He put up a hand and touched her throat with his fingers, lazily.

The idea he suggested, parking near the house in the car, the thought of the warm and dark interior and she and Skip enclosed in its privacy, filled Karen with a rush of almost dizzying sensations. A melting weakness poured through her. She nearly tottered, there against the wall with Skip's fingers touching her throat.

Then Skip muttered, "I've got to pick up a friend in metal class."

She was looking at him as if dazzled. "You mean someone's coming with us?" It didn't fit into the mental picture she had created; her thoughts whirled in confusion. But suddenly Skip moved off, taking her with him into the building. "Tell old man Pryde you've got a headache. I'll just walk out as if getting a drink of water or something. Meet you outside that door in thirty minutes."

She stumbled to her place, began mechanically working on the machine, meanwhile trying to sort sense from what Skip had told her. Under the emotional uproar she was aware of something else, a kind of dread at what she might be willing to do for Skip.

During the years of growing up which she had spent in the Havermann house, certain taboos had been instilled, not by anything as direct as spoken advice, since Mrs. Havermann never mentioned such things, nor lovingly by example, because temptation had no truck with that household, but rather by punctilious omission. Mrs. Havermann no longer lived in a world where people worried about anything more compelling than running out of sugar. Passion was a pale flare on the horizon of memory, growing dimmer year by year. The things she recalled from her marriage were the turmoil of its social obligations and the tantrums of her husband over his mislaundered shirts. And in some way of which both women were unconscious Mrs. Havermann had imposed her withdrawal upon the young girl.

Now Karen sat before a typewriter, the bulwarks trembling, and tried to force herself to be clear-headed, tried to keep from drowning in the emotional tide.

Skip meant to pick up a friend, she reminded herself. This must be Eddie, the one he had mentioned to her previously. Perhaps he just meant to give Eddie a lift first, before driving her home.

She wondered if Skip's friend would be able to see how

she felt, to sense the turmoil inside her. The thought was disturbing and at the same time steadying. She found herself drawing a deep, relaxing breath. What she felt for Skip was too strange, too raw and new, to be betrayed to anyone. It was a secret which she must keep to herself.

Skip parked the car by the curb and Eddie and Karen stepped out. All the way from school Karen had been puzzled and embarrassed, and Eddie knew it. He knew that she kept glancing at him as if wondering when he would leave them. On his part, Eddie wished in disgust that he had refused to return with Skip. Skip had a new air about him, and the way he drove and the way he whistled through his teeth told Eddie that he was feeling mean.

Skip came around the car, carrying the old blanket he used to cover the car's torn upholstery. "Let's go somewhere and talk," he said. Remembering what Skip had promised on the previous trip here, Eddie felt his face go tight and hot. He tried to mutter something about getting home, but Skip ignored it. Above them the trees climbed the rising ground, and all was as dark as a tomb.

Karen said in a shivery voice, "I thought we were going to sit in the car."

Skip gave an elaborate start of surprise. "Damned if we weren't. But it would be kind of crowded with Eddie in there, wouldn't it?" He walked uphill to the dark trees, the girl and Eddie following, and when he found an open spot he spread the blanket on the ground and flopped on it. There was nothing but a little starshine. Skip sighed and stretched out. "Come on, you two. Sit down."

Karen tucked in her skirt and sat down gingerly at the edge of the blanket. Eddie didn't sit down at all. He was beginning to get an idea that Skip was having a big joke here, that this amused him. He was tickled by their embarrassment and by their uncertainty over what he meant to do next. He felt that he held them in his power. He could do some outrageous thing, or nothing at all; it was just up to him.

"Sit down, Eddie. You're blocking the view."

Eddie said, "Ah, I'm not tired right now. I want to stretch my legs."

"Sit down anyway." The tone was a trifle ugly. Skip lay on his back and lit a cigarette and blew smoke at the sky. Eddie sat down. He could see the girl's face turned his way, a pale patch against the dark; he couldn't make out her eyes. He wondered what she was thinking, what she expected Skip to do. Around them the young trees whispered under a touch of wind, and there was a wild dusty smell. It was quiet, a long way from the city.

"Who's home at your place?" Skip asked all at once.

The girl didn't catch on at once; then she said, "You mean at Mrs. Havermann's?"

"Sure I mean at Mrs. Havermann's."

"Well, Mr. Stolz is there. He came this morning. There's her, and me, and that's all."

"How long is Stolz going to be there?"

"I don't know."

"Does he ever make a play for you, get fresh or funny, anything like that?"

"Why, of course he doesn't. He's real nice. You'd hardly

know he was in the house. He reads, or types in the library, or takes walks. He's friendly and . . . just sort of keeps to himself."

"Does he ever count his money where you can see him?"

Karen threw a glance toward Eddie; Eddie saw the quick turn of her head and sensed her eyes on him. She was beginning to realize that Skip was in an unpredictable mood; perhaps she was wondering, too, how much he had told Eddie. "No," she said uncertainly, "I've never seen the money."

"But you know it's there."

"Mrs. Havermann thinks it's there."

"*Thinks*?" Skip jerked himself indignantly up on one elbow. "Now wait a minute. What is this? You expect us to go ahead on just what the old woman thinks?"

"What do you mean, go ahead?" Her tone was scared, a scared whisper.

"Why, what we were talking about, how to get hold of some of that dough for ourselves," Skip said, maddeningly offhand. Eddie recognized the trick since Skip had played it a thousand times on him: delivering a jolt as if you were supposed to know all about it.

Karen seemed to huddle in the coat, shrinking down inside it. "You must be crazy, Skip. Just as crazy as can be."

Skip was bolt upright now, his manner angry and astounded. "You mean you've been feeding me a bunch of lies? It's all something you've made up in your head?"

He had confused her now. She said pleadingly, "You mistook what I said for something else. The money belongs to Mr. Stolz. He keeps it at Mrs. Havermann's place on account of some tax business."

"He's cheating the government," Skip pointed out nastily, "and he deserves to be cheated a little himself." It was infantile reasoning, but Skip put heat and conviction into it. "He's a crook. I ought to turn him in to the income-tax cops."

"Oh, don't do that!"

"I'm not going to. I just said I ought to. I'm going to help myself to some of the money; I'll let him pay me for keeping my mouth shut."

She sat so still, like a crouched animal, not saying anything, that Eddie knew she was afraid to have the conversation go on. She was afraid of what Skip would say next. At the same time she must have been doing some agonizing recapitulation, trying to recall all she had told him.

"We've got to make plans." Skip circled his knees with his arms, leaned his head on them as if thinking. "You'll have to find out exactly where the money is. Does he keep his room locked?"

"No, but I'm not supposed to ever go in there!" she cried.

"Where is his room?" He waited, and she said nothing, and Skip went on: "Upstairs? Near where you sleep?"

"No. Downstairs, next to the library. Oh, Skip, don't do this crazy thing!"

"Crazy, crazy, is that all you've got in your head?" He reached for her, pulled her nearer; she almost sprawled on her face. "It's up to you, this first part of it, finding the money and seeing how much it is, or a rough guess, and making sure we hit the place just after he's gone and when he won't be coming back for a while very soon. You get it?"

"I couldn't do it!"

"Chick, you've already done the main job, fingering the guy."

"What's that?"

"Letting somebody know who can use the information."

"I was just . . . talking. Passing time."

"Not with me you weren't." Her head was bent close and Skip was stroking her hair; Eddie could see the movement of his hand against her head. He heard crying, too. Karen was crying in desperate entreaty. "I like you a lot and you like me, and we can pull this off with Eddie here to help—"

"I'd have to leave home!" she wept.

"For Chrissakes, don't you want to? You want to live with that old dame, taking her charity, all your life?"

She hung there in silence, as if on the point of some terrible decision. "She's been awfully—"

"Good to you?" Skip mocked. "Treated you like a daughter?"

Skip's tone told Eddie this much: Skip knew Karen hadn't been treated as a daughter. For all that Skip had some sort of blind spot, unable to see himself, he could always pounce unerringly on the flaws in anyone else. Now he grabbed for Karen suddenly, pulled her over so that she lay across his knees, her shoulders against his chest. He looked at Eddie and said, "I'll meet you at the car."

Eddie got up and went quickly down through the trees. He felt an immense relief. There had been a moment when he had thought the girl wasn't going to co-operate, and he'd been afraid of what Skip might do to her. She was a kind of nice girl. Young and inexperienced. More than that, worse than that—ignorant. The girl was just ignorant enough to think Skip was interested in her instead of the money.

Eddie got into the car and put his head back and shut his eyes. He was half asleep when Skip came back alone. The girl had gone home by herself through the trees.

Skip got into the car, started the motor. He was grinning in the light from the dash, and his air was satisfied. The dog, he told Eddie, was a new arrival. Mrs. Havermann had taken it off the hands of a friend. It was just a pet, Karen said. "I think there's more to it," Skip concluded, "even if Karen doesn't know it. The old woman's nervous over all that money in the house. Bound to be."

They turned from the hillside roads into lower and shabbier streets, heading for home.

"It must be like sitting on a bomb," Skip said all at once, amused. "Yeah. Mrs. Havermann must feel that way." He drove as if musing over it. Eddie knew then that Skip was thinking of the old woman and her fear and of what sort of reaction she'd have on learning that someone else knew about the money and had come to get it.

CHAPTER THREE

Eddie let himself in quietly at the back door. The smells of the house swept over him, garlic and chili spices and stale coffee and an undefinable aroma of ingrained dirt. He stood still in the kitchen and listened. By now his dad should be asleep, fogged out on wine, but his mother might be up, reading or telling her beads. He had noted a light in the front room as he had come into the yard.

When he heard no sound, he went into the tiny hall and then on into the living room. His mother sat asleep in a chair, a magazine on her lap. She was a short, heavy woman, her neck thickened by a goiter, her gray hair thin and straggling. Her mouth had fallen open, and Eddie could see the gold tooth shining, the tooth put in in Mexico when she had been a girl.

As if his presence had signaled her sleeping mind, her eyes came open. They were large brown eyes, as gentle as a doe's; and Eddie never saw his mother's eyes without a recognition of the goodness, the loving charity within. She said sleepily, "Well, you're home now. Class was late a little?"

"A little." Eddie moved around the room to the door of his own room and stood awkwardly, wanting to go on in.

"Sit down, son."

There was a chair beside the door. It was springless, the arms mended with twined wire, a cushion covering the hole in its seat. "Yes, Mama, what is it?"

"I want to know about the class, how you're doing in it, what the teacher thinks of you." Her glance was pleased and eager.

"Oh, I'm doing all right. The teacher says I'm coming along."

"Today your father was talking to Mr. Arnold in the metal shop. Maybe you could go to work there, Eddie. Maybe the other thing, the trouble you've had, wouldn't stand in your way if you didn't mention it."

"Does Mr. Arnold know about my record?"

"No, I don't think so."

"He'd find out," Eddie said without bitterness.

"Well, it's a while yet before you finish the classes, isn't it? Maybe Mr. Arnold would let you help around the shop, not paying anything, until the class is done, and then he'd know what a good boy you are and he'd think the trouble didn't matter."

His mother was always planning these schemes for Eddie; he rejected this one without heat. Without hope, either. "Mama, the railroad doesn't let people come and work without paying them. And they don't take men with a police record, either. Dad's wasting his time talking to Arnold. Tell him to leave Arnold alone."

Her glance dropped from Eddie's face, settling on the magazine in her lap. "It seemed like such a fine idea."

"I know, Mama." Eddie avoided looking at his mother now. He knew that her life, hard as it was, and exposed to the violence of his father's drunkenness as it was, still protected her from many of the common cruelties and frustrations. She could not conceive of a few mistakes— as she thought of them, tolerantly—barring her son from a multitude of jobs. "We'll talk about it some other time. Maybe I'll come up with something of my own."

She spread her work-knotted hands on the cover of the magazine. "Yes. We'll think of something, you and I." She smiled gently. "You are too fine a boy not to have a fine job, Eddie." The glance she gave him was full of love. "Go to bed now. Don't worry, don't lie awake thinking about your troubles."

Eddie lay awake but briefly in the small overcrowded room. In those moments of wakefulness he thought of Skip and Skip's plan to rob the Havermann house of its store of money. Skip had talked of nothing else for more than a week. Karen seemed to be under his control now. Eddie allowed himself a brief wishful glimpse of riches, of buying a car for himself and something nice for his mother. A necklace, a nice dress, a big plastic purse like those in the fancy shopwindows. Maybe something for the house, too. To Eddie the house was familiar, its shabbiness acceptable; but he knew from remarks dropped now and then by his mother that she wanted the place fixed up. A new rug and a couple of chairs would bring a glow of joy to her brown eyes.

He woke in the early dawning, hearing his father pounding out to the kitchen, the rattle of glassware and the rush of water from the faucet. His father always downed about a pint of water before taking a pickup. Then he was ready for coffee, a couple of doughnuts, a second pickup, and so off to the job at the roundhouse.

Eddie's mother glanced in at him. She was huge inside the shapeless flannel gown, the gray hair tied up in skimpy braids, her enormous, bulbous throat hanging over the neck of the gown. "Cover up, Eddie. It's cool this morning."

He grunted, burrowing into the pillow. He went back to sleep. There was nothing to get up for. He'd given up hunting a job, even a temporary job to fill in until he was through the metalwork class, a long time ago.

Skip awoke in the room above the garage, raised himself on an elbow, and looked out at the morning. It was foggy, overcast, and a dull gray light lay over the neighborhood. Next to the garage was a big bank of shrubbery, then a plot of flowers, then the paved tennis court and the high brick wall surrounding the house next door. It was a district of once-exclusive homes now mostly broken up into housekeeping apartments and rooms-for-rent. Only a few of the original owners still lived here, among them Mr. Chilworth, who owned the big house at the front of the lot.

Skip sat up and rubbed the hair out of his eyes, yawned, put his bare feet on the floor. His uncle was already gone. He had made his bed on the other side of the room; it was neat and square under the white cotton counterpane. His uncle was probably already in the house now, cooking Mr.

Chilworth's breakfast. After cooking, and washing up the dishes, he'd start cleaning the house. In the afternoons his uncle worked in the garden. Mr. Chilworth was a bachelor, eighty-six years old, still hating women so badly he refused to keep a cleaning woman on the place. Skip's uncle performed as cook, maid, gardener, and chauffeur; and because Mr. Chilworth was practically impoverished now, the wages were poor, but Mr. Chilworth was broad-minded about a man with a prison record, and Skip's uncle had one. A long one.

Mr. Chilworth's charitable attitude was based in part upon the fact that there was nothing around worth stealing.

Skip went to the tiny bathroom and showered, brushed his teeth, shaved. He then looked over his uncle's shirts in the bureau drawer and chose one that he disliked less than the rest. His uncle was about his size, a slim wiry little man; he had Skip's foxy expression, though it was much subdued. He had learned to keep his eyes down. He walked with a shuffle. Mr. Chilworth's one complaint about his man of all work was that he came upon you silently, without warning. At first, seven months ago, Mr. Chilworth had found it annoying.

When Skip was through dressing, he went down the outer staircase to the yard, through the yard to the rear door of the big house. Here was a large screened porch, on it some of the overflow from the kitchen, boxes of pots and pans no longer needed, cases of health food and vegetable juices, an old refrigerator minus its door where Mr. Chilworth kept oranges and grapefruit. Skip went through to the enormous kitchen. His uncle Willy was sitting at a breadboard pulled out from the cabinet, drinking coffee and reading a racing sheet. Uncle Willy nodded without speaking. His gaze lingered for a moment on his shirt.

"How's for breakfast?" said Skip, the usual greeting.

Skip's uncle rose and went to the stove and lit a fire under a skillet. It had already been used for Mr. Chilworth's meal and had some scraps of egg in the bottom. Uncle Willy broke two eggs in a bowl, beat them with a fork, grated some cheese over them, added a dollop of cream, dumped the whole into the pan. "Watch it," he said, going back to his stool by the breadboard.

Skip whistled between his teeth, stirring the eggs with the fork with which Uncle Willy had beaten them. When the mass congealed, he pushed it out upon a plate, salted it, took it to the sinkboard near his uncle. His uncle meanwhile had shoved a piece of bread in the toaster and poured a second cup full of coffee. Skip ate standing. "What looks good today?"

His uncle grunted, sucked his teeth with an air of disgust, folded the racing sheet, and tossed it over.

"When's he going to let you go out there?"

Uncle Willy shrugged, implying that Mr. Chilworth hadn't said when he might take an afternoon off for the races.

"Well, when did you go last?" Skip asked.

"Three weeks."

Skip considered. "You know, this isn't much of a job you've got here, Unc. The wages are nothing. You scrub and wash, mow the lawn and dig crab grass, and he doesn't even give you a day off for the races."

Uncle Willy waited for a moment before answering. "I'm eating. So are you," he pointed out with a dry air.

"So? It's not hard to eat now. Times are pretty good. Even the panhandlers are fat. For what you do here, working your tail off from morning to night, you ought to do better."

"You know where I can do better?" Uncle Willy asked mildly.

"An experienced man like you," Skip added with a side-long glance.

An oddly quiet and attentive look came over his uncle. He put down the cup of coffee and regarded Skip for a moment in silence. The buzzing of a fly on the pane over the sink was the only sound in the room.

Skip said, "How old are you now? Fifty? By now you must have caught on to a lot of angles."

"I might have." Under the attentive expression was a sort of question.

"What were you in for?"

"I don't want to talk about that, Skip. One thing I've learned here, learned from Mr. Chilworth, is that the past is as dead as you let it be. And I want mine to be really forgotten."

Skip nodded indifferently. "Sure. You're right." He seemed ready to abandon the line of conversation.

"I made my mistakes, just as you did, Skip; but we both paid for them with time out of our lives. You're lucky, you're young, you haven't lost all the middle years." The tone had the air of sermon in it, but Uncle Willy's eyes had taken on a certain sharpness. He studied Skip warily, prying at him with little glances.

"Just blowing off my big mouth," Skip said apologetically.

"Nothing specific in mind?"

"No, not a thing."

When he had finished eating Skip went back to the room above the garage, threw the bedding together, and flopped on the bed. He had some planning to do; he had to get to Las Vegas by the day after tomorrow, when Karen said that Stolz would probably return. His jalopp would never hold up for such a grind. He considered going by bus; but though the fare would only be a little over fifteen dollars roundtrip, Skip had little hope of getting the amount out of his uncle. Karen either. Old lady Havermann kept her on nickels and dimes. The answer, obviously, was to hitch-hike. Take a local bus for two bits, get as far out on the highway as possible, use his thumb. The prospect bored him, but getting to Las Vegas and checking on Stolz was a necessary precaution. Skip was innately suspicious.

When Skip was fifteen he'd been arrested for the first time for driving a stolen car. The car had been loaned him by a school friend who had been positive it belonged to his old maid aunt, who didn't mind who drove it. In this way Skip got his name in the police records, and he learned distrust. Before he did anything about the money in the Havermann house he intended to check its source.

It was one thing to rob an old woman who would start screaming for the cops, and another to steal from a gambler hiding his dough from Uncle Whiskers and the tax collectors.

He had also to think up an excuse to give to the typing teacher and the bookkeeping teacher for a two- or three-day absence. In spite of what he had told Karen, he had no intention of giving up the classes until the other thing had been accomplished and the money was in his possession. Uncle Willy only allowed him to stay here sharing Mr. Chilworth's spare bounty because he was learning a trade.

He decided to palm off a story on the teachers about his brother in Fresno, sick, wanted to see him. Skip had a brother who lived near Fresno, ran a vineyard, a winery and a fig orchard, and, sick or well, wouldn't want anything further to do with him. He had a Presbyterian wife and three kids. The whole family was, in Skip's opinion, fantastically law-abiding.

Skip was digging in the closet for a zipper bag he recalled having seen there when he heard his uncle come softly up the stairs and into the room. "Skip? You in here?"

Skip backed from the closet, the dusty bag in his hand. "Yeah. Look, do you mind if I use this for a couple of days?"

His uncle studied the bag. "Why do you want it?"

"I'm going to make a short trip, need it for shaving stuff and so on." Skip knew from experience that a hitchhiker with any sort of luggage had a better chance of getting a ride than one without. The one without had a look of footloose mischief from which most drivers shied away. A bag, even a small one, implied possessions and a destination.

"Where are you going?"

"Oh, not too far," Skip said vaguely, unzipping the bag and glancing into it.

"You're giving up your classes?" Skip's uncle went to his bed across the room and sat down lightly on its edge. For the first time Skip noted the steadily attentive manner;

it made him uneasy. "I don't think that would be the wise thing to do. Learning is money, Skip. It enables you to rise above the common herd. Look at me, grammar grade education, prison record; all I can get is the kind of slavery I do here. Work that nobody else would take." His prying eyes were full of questions.

"Education isn't the only thing," Skip muttered.

"Well, what else is there?"

"A break."

"You're getting a break somehow? This trip is a break?"

Skip felt that his uncle's persistence was drawing from him things he would have preferred not to divulge. He saw where that moment of incaution in the kitchen, that desire to hint and boast, had led. He looked at his uncle. "I can't talk about it."

"I think you'd better."

"Huh?"

"I think you'd better explain. I'm real curious about this trip and whatever else you're planning. And then, too, I might be able to give you some advice."

Skip thought about it while he took a soiled shirt off a hook and dusted out the interior of the bag. His uncle had not been a successful thief, though he had once had the reputation of moving with a big-time mob. Long prison sentences had sapped his body, curdled his manner into silent submission, slowed his walk to a shuffle. "Ah, there's nothing you could tell me."

"Maybe not. Maybe so. Who's in this with you?"

"Who's in what?"

"This break you're talking about."

They were circling verbally. Skip wished he had made up a story for Uncle Willy, something like being invited to stay with Eddie for a couple of days. "Oh, a guy I know."

"Eddie Barrett?"

"Yeah." Skip threw the dirty shirt into a hamper in the bathroom, came out, began to look around for something to stick into the bag. There was no need to pack yet, but he didn't want to have to sit down and face Uncle Willy and parry his questions.

Uncle Willy sat in silence as if thinking. Finally he said, "Is it a big thing? Something worth taking a risk for?" When Skip didn't answer he went on, "Because Eddie might not be up to it. There might be a catch somewhere and Eddie could let you down."

"Eddie's okay." Skip shrugged it off. "Anyway, he's not carrying the ball. I am. It's my baby."

"In any job," said Uncle Willy, "the least man, the man with almost nothing to do, can bitch you up. That's what happened to me, that's why I'm a two-time loser. That's why, even if you told me all about it, I couldn't go in with you or have the least thing to do with it."

Skip said, "That's right, you couldn't. Three times and you're out."

"So you can tell me whatever you want." Uncle Willy moistened his lips. "I can say what I think and that's all. Right now I'm telling you, watch Eddie Barrett. He's a punk kid in a lot of ways."

"Yeah, maybe you've got something there." Skip went into the bathroom and inspected his meager array of shaving stuff, as if making a note of what he needed to take.

"Now, where's this trip you're taking?"

"Las Vegas." In an expansive mood, Skip began to tell Uncle Willy about Stolz and the money in old lady Havermann's house.

CHAPTER FOUR

"Who is this girl, this Karen Miller?" Uncle Willy wanted to know.

"Old Mrs. Havermann never adopted her legally. Karen's dad was a friend of Mr. Havermann in the old days before he made his money, and when Miller died Karen was left all alone, an orphan kid about ten years old, and the Havermanns took her in. Havermann died about a year later. Karen stayed on with the old woman, helped with the housework for her keep."

"How does the old lady treat her?"

"Okay, I guess. Hell, she's not her mother. She wants Karen to earn what she hands out to her."

"No animosity there, you think?"

"No, Karen likes the old woman."

"How does Stolz fit into the picture?"

"He was married to Mrs. Havermann's daughter. They were divorced. The daughter–she's around thirty, I guess –she lives back East somewhere. The old woman stayed friends with Stolz. Maybe he pays her something, I don't know. Karen doesn't think so. She thinks the old woman is kind of sweet on Stolz even if he is about fifteen years younger than her."

Uncle Willy sucked his teeth and twiddled his thumbs thoughtfully. "You were right about going to check up in Las Vegas. That's the thing to do. Make sure. You got a good look at Stolz through the window?"

"Ah, I'd know him anywhere," Skip said.

"When are you leaving?"

"Day after tomorrow. That's when Stolz is supposed to go. Karen will let me know for sure, of course, when it happens."

"You might not run into him over there, you might have to inquire around, and you'd better handle that pretty carefully. Some of those boys in Nevada own those clubs sort of under the counter, so to speak. Silent partners. There's a reason. Nobody with a record is supposed to have any piece of the gambling over there."

"For Chrissakes, you think I'm a nut or something?"

"It takes thinking about, more than you might realize."

"I'll do okay."

Skip came out of the bus depot, into the bright hot Nevada sunlight, and looked around for a cab to take him out to the Strip. Karen was sure that Stolz would be there by now, in one of the big hotels. She was sure that he had nothing to do with any of the downtown clubs, catering to the less-well-heeled and the more transient suckers. Old Mrs. Havermann and Stolz had never mentioned the name of the hotel where he was supposed to live and in which he

had a share, but Skip and Uncle Willy had done a little figuring. Stolz had been coming to Mrs. Havermann's house
off and on for a little more than three years, according to
Karen's memory, and it would seem logical that he had ac-
quired his gambling interests at about that time. Several of
the biggest and most lavish hotels had opened since then,
and these could be ignored, provided Stolz hadn't switched
his investment.

Uncle Willy thought it most likely that Stolz had bought
into one of the older establishments. He had telephoned a
friend who had Nevada contacts, and from the friend had
obtained a list of probabilities. Skip carried the list in his
pocket, along with the return bus ticket financed by Uncle
Willy in a burst of generosity.

When a cab drew in to the curb, Skip read off the name
of the first hotel on the list; the cabbie nodded. They
rapidly left the downtown area for through boulevards
heading west. Skip had been through Las Vegas several
times. He was always interested, when passing through
the Strip, to see the new hotels which were constantly being added to the long line on either side of the highway
stretching toward Los Angeles. Great piles of million-
dollar masonry, glass and brick, they rose like fantastic
palaces set amid tropic gardens. He read the names: the
Sands, the Sahara, the Flamingo, Desert Inn, the Dunes,
Thunderbird; and the vision of their opulence filled him
with excitement. Only the knowledge of his own flattened
wallet kept him from vainglorious dreams.

By seven that evening he was in the third hotel of the
list Uncle Willy had prepared, and getting nowhere. He

had found himself the recipient of cool evaluation by pit bosses, room clerks, and bar waitresses. Skip had no money to spend; he could only look. He knew that the category *flat broke* was pinned on him by the dealers within ten minutes of his entering the casinos. A stubborn anger had begun to burn.

He was at a crap table. The dice were in the hands of a thickset man with an alcohol flush, expensive clothes, diamond stickpin and solitaire. Two blond chippies clung to him, slipping ten-dollar chips into their gilt bags when opportunity presented. The man was loud, much the worse for liquor, and held up the game for long periods while he argued with one or both of the girls. What Skip took in was the attitude of the dealers at the table, the hovering pit boss: they wore fixed smiles and they ignored or pacified complaints from other players. Plainly here was big money working.

He waited and watched the stack of chips dwindle. All at once he found the man staring at him across the crap table.

"Hey, you?"

Skip was stupefied. "Who?"

"You. Young fella. You come around here." He beckoned with a weaving arm. Skip looked around, too dumfounded to know what to do. He caught the eye of the pit boss, the faint nod that commanded him to obey. Skip went around the table and the old man pushed one of the chippies away roughly and pulled Skip in close. "Uh-huh. You remind me of my boy. Did remind me. I mean, he used to look like you." The thickset man hiccuped loudly. "Foxy boy. In England now. Long way off." He was fumbling chips and pushing them into Skip's hands.

Skip wanted to stare at them; he knew they were worth ten dollars apiece and the old man had given him more than a dozen.

"Play 'em," the thickset man commanded.

Skip put one down tentatively; the old man shot the dice; the dealer raked in the bets. The old man had brought in a two-spot, craps. Skip put down another chip.

"Naw," the old man said. "Lookee here. Fix 'em up. You get nowhere piddling along." He raked Skip's hands clean and dribbled the orange chips across the green felt, betting the line, the big six and eight, come bets, everything. Skip's brief riches were all spread out waiting for the throw. Skip felt breath die out in his lungs, his heart's thumping. Maybe . . .

Craps again. The old man had neglected that particular item. Skip stepped back into the shadows, expecting to be dismissed, but the old man turned bloodshot eyes to search him out. "Hey, you!"

The chippie was staring into Skip's face as if the least thing would set her to clawing his eyes. "I'm . . . I'm broke," Skip muttered.

"Sure. Sure. I've been broke a million times," the old man boomed. "Had to clean spittoons in Fairbanks, Alaska. Drove a mule team between Barstow and Daggett—one hundred and ten in the shade and there wasn't any shade. Never knew what it was in the sun. Afeared to look." He was throwing bills across the green felt to the dealer, who poked them into a slot in the table and replaced them with more orange chips. "What you want to remember, boy —luck's gonna change. Nobody ever has bad luck all the time."

Skip wanted to say, "You sure about it?" but he held his tongue. The old man had pulled him back to the table, given him a double fistful of the chips and was telling him how to play. Skip glanced at his shoulder, feeling pressure there. A girl's palm was outspread. Skip shrugged and turned away. The girl said, "You little son of a bitch!"

"Get lost."

"You'd better stay away from Mr. Salvatorre! These people at the hotel keep an eye on him!" she hissed at him.

"They'd better watch you," Skip told her.

She didn't leave. He was aware of her warm flesh, the perfume, the silver glitter of her hair. She had on a red sheath dress, cut so tight Skip didn't understand how she could breathe. She wore a clutter of platinum bangles on her wrists. Her bare legs above gold sandals were chocolate-colored from the sun. "Nasty little man. You belong on skid row. Why don't you go away and quit trying to crash the party?"

Skip didn't answer. He was interested in what was happening to his money. The old man had given him over two hundred dollars, and now by a rapid calculation he found that he was down to eighty.

"Play up, boy, play up!" The old man leaned his belly on the rim of the table and chanted to the dice. Afterward he bought more chips.

An ugly feeling of disappointment surged through Skip. He wasn't going to come out of this with anything. It was a con game, a racket. The old fool must be a shill, playing on house money. Or else he was a nut. Skip was himself too unpredictable and too insecure to endure eccentricity in others.

He was trying desperately to think of a way to back off with even a few of the chips left when Salvatorre suddenly decided he'd had enough of dice. Now it was time to try the slot machines. He dragged Skip along to another part of the big casino, ordered drinks for everybody in sight, passing out quarters and half dollars as fast as he could buy them from the change girl. The two blondes made Skip think of hovering vultures. They did everything but crawl into Salvatorre's pockets. Skip noted that very little of what the old man gave them went into the machines. They rapidly switched the change back into bills and tucked the bills away into the bulging gilt bags.

The tempo around Salvatorre increased. The old man was almost in a frenzy. He had a half dozen slots going, was stuffing change into the girls' hands and tossing Skip an occasional batch of quarters. Skip noticed that the pit boss in the distance was keeping an eye on things. It could be true that the old man was a valued and familiar patron.

All at once Mr. Salvatorre was staring into his empty hands in a way that was almost tearful. "Broke. I'm broke, boy," he cried to Skip.

It was crazy. Skip knew that Salvatorre still had money in his wallet. One of the change girls glided up, smiling, to say, "Why, we'd be pleased to cash a check for you, Mr. Salvatorre."

All around them the slots were clanging; Salvatorre shook his head as if unable to hear. She repeated what she had just said, but Salvatorre blinked his eyes sadly. "Broke. Going to call it a night." He glanced around, noticed the bright-eyed chippie in the red sheath, saw Skip in the shadows. "We'll have a nightcap, the three of us. Come on, we'll go up to my room now; you'll order whatever you want."

Skip was wary, more than half disgusted. He saw the girl throw a victorious cat-smile at the other chippie, who appeared to take it philosophically and began to inspect the loot in her handbag. The girl in red then snatched Salvatorre's arm. "Not him," she mouthed, nodding toward Skip. "Let's leave him out of it."

It would have suited Skip; he had four or five dollars in quarters and half dollars and two ten-dollar chips. He had no desire to get better acquainted with the eccentric old man.

But Salvatorre roared a protest, threatening to dislodge the chippie on his arm. "Leave him here? Course not! Going to buy the boy a drink. Makes me think of my boy Al, over in England. Foxy boy, good boy, needs a drink."

"Tell him you're under age, darling," the blonde purred to Skip.

"Twenty-two," Skip said, unwilling to oblige her.

She showed her teeth at him.

The three of them went from the casino into the huge lobby. Outside, beyond great glass doors, was the pool, lit with pink light at its edges, surrounded by late swimmers and a few diners at the little tables in the dusky distance. Inside here was an air of carpeted quiet and the watchful eyes of two clerks at a desk in a niche across the way. Skip knew their gaze was for him, and he tensed with a sense of danger. The girl, that was expected, but they had cold stares for Skip. He might be up to something with their valuable Mr. Salvatorre, who had just provided a good chunk of the overhead for the day.

Skip stared back in defiance, but his heart wasn't in it. There was power here, concealed, it was true, under a show of hospitality, but nevertheless capable of swift and ruthless action. He had no illusions as to what would happen to him if he should try to slip off, say, with an added chunk of Mr. Salvatorre's money.

In Mr. Salvatorre's room the air-conditioning ducts hummed softly. There were flowers, bottles of good wine, a tray of snacks. Salvatorre ignored all this and rang for room service. The waiter came so quickly that Skip wondered if he had been stationed in the hall. "Drinks!" Mr. Salvatorre commanded, motioning toward the girl on the couch and Skip standing over by the windows.

The waiter looked patient and obedient; his attitude was one of simple politeness and not that of the cold hostility of the desk men.

"A stinger," the blonde said languidly, stroking the fat side of the gilt handbag.

"A double Scotch with water back," said Skip.

"Good boy!" the old man approved. "That's what my Al would say. And waiter, I want Irish whiskey with Coca-Cola in it."

Now that's a drink for you, Skip thought in distaste. He listened to the sounds from outside, where swimmers were splashing in the pool and a girl was laughing in a high-pitched squeal. He thought of the old dun-colored house, Uncle Willy's garage apartment, Mr. Chilworth and the amount of work he got from Uncle Willy for practically nothing; and he looked with disbelieving eyes on Salvatorre. How did a crazy old man like this acquire so much money?

He said tentatively, "You made it in mining, I'll bet."

"Some in mining," said Salvatorre, nodding his head, sitting down by the blonde and playfully squeezing her knee through the red sheath dress. "Some in oil. All by accident, boy. A man owed me some debts and all he owned, all he had left, was some desert land out in the middle of nowhere. Worth nothing. So he gave it to me and I forgot it and I went on working until five years ago. Then came the oil. I was a butcher for more than thirty years." He looked the girl over, as if she were some toy he meant to see perform before the evening was over. The blonde had taken a tiny vial of perfume from the overstuffed bag and was dabbing her ears and her palms with scent.

Skip thought, now why in hell couldn't something like that have happened to Uncle Willy? Uncle Willy had spent his years desperately planning how to scrounge a little money here and there, and being sent to prison for his efforts, and here was this stupid old coot who'd had it handed to him, who'd done nothing. The unfairness of it was stupefying.

The waiter brought the drinks. Salvatorre paid him and

ordered refills at once, before they had even started on the
first ones. Skip sat and drank, trying not to look very often at the couch. It was embarrassing, the old man almost
paralyzed with booze and the skillful and willing chippie,
whose skill and willingness weren't enough. Presently
Skip took his drink into the bathroom and stayed there a
long time. He heard the second arrival and departure of
the waiter. Finally he went back into the other room. The
sight he saw was curious.

Salvatorre lay stretched out on his back on the couch,
obviously dead to the world. The blonde was at the dresser,
fluffing her hair with a little silver comb. "Hi," she said to
Skip. There was no animosity in her now. She winked at
him in the mirror. "I'm going back to the casino. He'll be
passed out for hours." She slipped the comb back into the
purse and Skip saw the enormous roll of bills.

"Give me some," he said.

She crinkled her nose at him. "Oh, now, let's be realistic."

"You didn't give him anything for his money," Skip per-
sisted, "because he was too drunk to take it. You've charged
him for nothing. I want a cut of it."

She adjusted the neck of the sheath, tucking it a little
lower over her sharply pointed breasts. "Don't get funny
here, lover boy. You'd better take your small change and
blow. The management will be along pretty soon to look
Mr. Salvatorre over and maybe put him to beddy-bye. And
they'll kick you out then if you haven't already gone."

Skip stepped close and put a hand at the back of her neck,
where the skull joined the fragile spine, and he closed his
fingers slowly. She tried to lunge forward, out of his grip,

but the dresser held her. Then she tried to twist sidewise and away and Skip put an arm tight around her waist. He went on pinching the base of her skull and she turned white and started to scream and he lifted his free hand and slapped her hard. "Give," he said. He let up on the pressure at her neck and her head sagged forward drunkenly.

"My head! My head!" she moaned.

"It'll ache a little," he agreed. He pushed her aside and inched his fingers into her purse and extracted a chunk of money.

"Don't . . . take it all!"

"I'm not. I'm leaving you plenty."

He had a bad moment when he opened the hall door. A big man stood there, beefy inside a neat blue suit, hands like slabs of granite, a cold green eye. Skip repressed a start of fright. He said quietly, "I'm just leaving."

"Fine," said the man with the green eyes. He looked inside the room at the girl in front of the dresser. "You leaving too, Tina?"

"Yes, I'm leaving," Tina got out.

The big man waited, intending to see that Mr. Salvatorre was comfortable and alone. Skip started down the hall, and then from nowhere at all came a curious hunch, a thing to say. He obeyed it instinctively. He paused and looked back at the beefy man in Salvatorre's doorway. "I don't suppose it means anything."

"What's that?"

"What Mr. Salvatorre was telling me. He said if I wanted a job here in Las Vegas, he'd speak to somebody he called Mr. Stolz."

No change in the green eyes or the patient manner; the beefy man looked at Skip as from a vast distance, somebody looking at nobody, or a man on a curb watching a bit of trash blow by in the gutter.

"This . . . this Stolz. Is he anybody?"

The granite lips parted. "Mr. Stolz has retired for the evening. If I were you I wouldn't try to come back to see him. Mr. Salvatorre might not recall what he promised to do."

"Mr. Stolz owns the hotel?"

"A partner." The beefy man turned away to look at Tina inside the room.

Skip went away, through the lobby and into the desert night outside. He looked for a cab. In a freakish way he could never have foreseen he had found out about Stolz and made a little money into the bargain.

CHAPTER FIVE

Uncle Willy got off the bus in Beverly Hills and walked two blocks north of Sunset, up the hill where the big homes and apartment houses towered perchlike against the sky. He entered a small open courtyard. The low one-storied building surrounded it on three sides. There was a great deal of tropical shrubbery and a tiny fountain in a copper bowl. On the left was the door of a dentist's office, to the right were a couple of doctors. In the rear, beyond a screen of bougainvillea, was a door on which, in gilt letters, was printed R. Mocksly Snope, Attorney At Law. Uncle Willy crossed the courtyard and entered.

An artfully cosmeticked redhead in a tan sleeveless dress was seated in the outer office. The thing she was seated behind might have been a desk or it might have been a slab of metallic substance which had fallen through the roof off an airplane; Uncle Willy couldn't make up his mind which.

"Yes, sir?" The smile was careful, the eyes amused.

"I'd like to see Mr. Snope."

"Do you have an appointment, sir?" She clipped legal-sized pages together and stacked them at the edge of the metallic structure before her.

"No. Just tell him it's Willy Dolman. He knows me."

"Mr. Snope is very busy today."

"I'll wait." Uncle Willy looked around for a chair and found some contorted steel tubing and black plastic foam. He sat down. The thing fitted you strangely close, he thought, once you got into it.

She lifted a section of the metallic desk and peered into it, as if she might have a cake baking inside; then she spoke, softly inaudible words and afterward she listened. Then she looked in surprise at Willy.

"Mr. Snope will see you now," she said, as if she could scarcely believe it. She rose and walked to a door and opened it. Uncle Willy, with his hat in his hands, went on in. Snope was grinning at him from the other side of the room. Snope's carpet was a deep garnet red and his desk had no resemblance to a wing fallen off a plane; it was solid mahogany, six feet across, and shone like a mirror.

"Well, long time no see. Have a chair," Snope said, and opened a leather box and offered Willy a cigar.

Snope was about sixty, a stout man with a ruddy skin. He wore a gray hard-weave suit which must have cost around three hundred dollars in Willy's opinion. There was a pe-culiarity about Snope; in spite of his obvious age he had a certain juvenile softness and cheerfulness, an odd inno-cence, considering his class of clients and the seamy side of the legal profession he practiced.

"I was glad to hear you were out, Willy. How are things with you?"

"Not too bad." Willy explained about Mr. Chilworth and his job.

"Well, that's fine." Snope lit their cigars with a silver lighter. "I'm glad to know that you've settled down and aren't planning any more mischief."

"I'm settled down, all right," Willy said.

"You were a good man, a clever man, in your day. But we all get old. We all get to a certain point, and then it's time to take stock and think a bit and figure what the odds are. Sometimes the odds are such that we have to quit taking chances." Under Snope's mild tone was a warning, and Willy sensed it.

"I know I'm too old to plan any more jobs. I haven't any ideas along that line at all."

"Fine, fine. You're looking well, too. Taking on a little tan."

"That's the yard work," Willy explained. "What I came about is something else entirely. Not a job of mine. It's one I got wind of by accident."

Snope's face closed coldly and he inspected the cigar as if he thought it might harbor some species of insect life. "Now . . . Willy, I've advised you to the best of my knowledge—"

"It's not *my* job," Willy insisted. "I wouldn't touch it, in fact. But the thing is, the people who are planning it are punks. They don't know how to organize. It's going to sky-rocket unless somebody with know-how takes over." He waited, a careful moment. "If someone with experience, the right person, got into it there might be a big payoff."

There was a tick-tock of such silence that Willy could hear Miss Redhead typing rattledy-clack in the outer office.

"Well, then—" Snope put his cigar into a crystal ash tray and stuck his hands palm down on the desk. His mouth had tightened. "Whom do you want to see?"

"I thought, well . . . Big Tom, if he isn't too busy."

"Big Tom." Snope thought about Big Tom, revolved Big Tom in his brain and inspected him from various angles. "It's his kind of job?"

"No."

Snope allowed a touch of suspicion to come up under the juvenile cheer, and Willy saw as usual and with the usual surprise that the youthful optimism was as false, really, as Mr. Snope's beautiful white teeth.

"I owe Big Tom a favor," Willy explained. "I've waited a long time to pay off. You know, when that last job went sour, when we were keeping our heads down and the heat was so bad we could hardly breathe, it was Big Tom did me a good turn. He loaned me a car and some money and it was just chance he didn't get pinched over it."

"I see." Snope twiddled his fingers on the mahogany. Then he said abruptly, "How big?"

"I don't know that yet."

"Will you know it before you pull the job?"

"Hope to."

Snope nodded. He had said nothing yet about his cut; and Willy understood that this was taken for granted. Snope got up from his chair and went to a steel file cabinet and extracted a folder. He studied the folder for a while; it contained some items about car accident statistics and the legal settlement of the same, but Mr. Snope seemed to be reading between the lines. After a while he said, "All right. Here's the address."

Willy copied down what Snope told him.

Snope laid the folder on his desk. "How many more?"

"I'll let Big Tom handle it."

Snope nodded. "Fine." He was smiling youthfully, his manner full of boyish good will. "Leave a phone number with Miss Weems. Don't call me, I'll call you." On the way to the door he clapped Willy cheerfully on the shoulders.

There was wind in the canyon, the smell of sage and syc-amores, the old dry taste of summer dust, heat, a muffled quiet. Uncle Willy paused on the rutted road to wipe the sweat off his face with his handkerchief. He hated not having a car. Being afoot in southern California meant de-pending on a public transportation system which would have been insufficient for 1890.

Above him a pink-trimmed cabin peeped from a grove of trees. Uncle Willy looked up at it, narrowing his eyes against the glare. Steps led up from the unpaved road. There were patches of ivy and geraniums on the slope, and, seeing these, a look of recognition flickered in Willy's eyes. Big Tom had always been great for gardening. Gar-dens and cats. Sure enough, there was a big yellow cat on the porch above, looking down at Willy with the air of watching a mouse.

Willy climbed the steps, went up on the porch, rapped at the door. It wasn't a big place, but there was a great deal of privacy. From the porch there were no other houses visible, just the road leading off into the lonely sunlight. Willy heard a stir in the room, steps, then the door opened before him. "Hi, you old son of a gun," Willy said, and the man inside let forth a great cackle of laughter.

"Well, for God's sake, look who's here!"

Big Tom wore a pair of jeans and a knitted white tee shirt. His big toes were hooked into rubber sandals. He had a great mane of gray hair, stiff as wire, pale skin matted with freckles, a broad face, a heavy mouth. He was fat now; Willy commented at once upon how much fatter Big Tom was than when he had last seen him.

"Hell, you were salted away a long time, Willy!" They were seated by now. Big Tom gazed suddenly at Willy with his hazel-colored eyes. "Who gave you the address here?"

"Snope."

"What the hell were you doing with him?" Then an air, quiet and watchful, settled over Big Tom. "Wait a minute. You've come on business?" Big Tom shook his head decisively. "Afraid you're barking up the wrong tree. Don't plan on me, Willy. I'm all through."

Willy nodded mildly. "I know, it's not even your kind of job. I wanted to offer it, though, because of the favors you did me in the past."

"Forget it." Big Tom turned the talk to other subjects: the house, the yard and the flowers, his family of cats. They were outdoors presently and Big Tom led Willy toward the lath house. "Begonias in here. I'm slipping some gardenias and camellias—not hard to do, but it takes them forever to start growing. See this fern? Jap gave it to me. The Japs

58

irradiate or poison the damned fern some way; it comes all crinkly like that, like green lace."

Willy nodded over the ferns. He thought the place smelled mossy and fungus-like. He said, "There's this guy from Vegas, owns a chunk of a hotel over there. He's got some dough hid out in an old barn of a place in Pasadena. Nobody around but an old woman and a young girl. The girl won't make any trouble."

Big Tom rearranged some potted plants and ran a hose over some fuchsias. "I'm sorry to hear that you're meddling around with such things, Willy. You know and I know that you can't afford it."

"I'm not going to have any part of it," Willy said. "I'm just offering you the information because you tried to help me a long time ago when nobody else would have spit on me if I was afire."

Big Tom thrust a finger into a basket. "Getting dry. That's the trouble with the canyon, the wind through here drying everything out. I water these fuchsias three, four times a day. Can't keep 'em damp otherwise. Not even here, under the lath." He worked his way around the bench.

"You always went for this stuff," said Willy, trying not to walk on the fine green creeping growth on the floor.

"I'd of sure been better off if I'd done what the old gardener wanted me to. You know, that first time I was inside –they let me help Mr. Wilcox and he taught me to garden and grow things. Vegetables, too, that was the work end of it; we had to supply the tables at Preston. Then the flowers –he showed me how–that was the fun end of it, the beauty end, and I almost got a job gardening when I got out. Only, there was my brother. You remember Buddy."

"Yeah. I remember."

Two yellow cats came in and rubbed themselves against Big Tom's legs. Big Tom shoved them off with his toe. "If I had gone to gardening after that first hitch, it would have changed my whole life." He mused over some begonias with reddish hairy leaves and a long spate of crimson bloom. He said, "What's Snope want out of it?"

"He'll want the usual ten per cent."

"What do you want?"

"I'll settle for the same. Ten."

"That's not much."

"If what I think is there is there, it could be plenty. A half million wouldn't surprise me none. Look, this has been going on for more than three years. You know the kind of lettuce they cut over there in Nevada."

"Could be."

Willy's eyes had begun to gleam. He had a sudden vivid picture of himself at the track. The horses were parading to the post. He was all dressed up, and there was a wad of money in his hand. He'd just cashed a slew of tickets on a fifteen-to-one shot. Willy grew so excited under the compelling reality of the dream that he could scarcely stand still.

Big Tom was studying quietly over something. "What's been done so far?"

"My punk nephew got acquainted with the girl. She just lives there, works for her keep. She told him about this guy named Stolz and the money. Skip's got some wild idea he can pull it off with the help of another punk named Eddie

Barrett. Believe me, this Eddie is from nothing. It's going to fall on their heads."

"Maybe not."

"Chrissakes, they don't know anything!" Willy cried. "They think they'll walk in there and tie up the old woman and heist the dough and take the girl with them when they walk out. Just like that!"

"They might get away with it," Big Tom said.

"Look. If Stolz is big in Nevada, he'll have connections here. Hot ones. You think he'll sit still for it? Nuts." Willy almost backed into the ferns. "He'll peg out their hides in his lobby, that's what he'll do."

Big Tom said, "Well, let's go inside and have a beer. We'll talk it over. Before I'd go ahead with it I'd have to know more about the money."

"The girl's going to find out about that."

"You've met her?"

"Never. Don't intend to. That's what I mean about these punks not knowing anything. They're careless; they even drive around and look the place over by daylight; they run around with the girl."

Big Tom led the way back, shaking his head sadly.

Eddie went into the kitchen and looked into the coffeepot. There was a dark greasy cupful swimming in the bottom. He turned the gas on under it. From his mother's room he heard the creak of bedsprings.

"Eddie? You're up? You want something to eat?"

"I'll get it, Ma."

"Tortillas in the oven, beans on the stove."

"I want some eggs."

"In the icebox." She was in there resting, Eddie knew. Her heart bothered her a lot; she was short of breath, needed an operation for the goiter. The first thing I do, Eddie thought, thinking of the money—the first thing is the operation. Then some clothes for her, a good coat, maybe a fur one.

He saw his father's wine bottle on the sink and said to himself, For him, a kick in the guts.

He was frying the eggs when he heard her in the doorway and looked around. She had on a blue cotton house dress, bedroom slippers, an old green wool sweater thrown across her shoulders. "Eddie, I've been thinking. You know, about the job you might get with Mr. Arnold."

"Arnold doesn't do the hiring, Mama. He just works for the railroad like anybody else. Sure he's a straw boss, over the metal-shop, but it doesn't mean he could recommend me or anything. I'd have to fill out an application at the office and put down everything I've ever done. Including time I've served, and that would let me out right there."

He saw her desperate anxiety and pleading but closed his mind to it. "Sometimes I get scared. I think maybe you'll do something you shouldn't, maybe get into trouble again." She tried to pry into his closed face.

"I'm okay. I'm studying, I'll find something. They need metalmen. Even with records, they need them."

"Sure." The smile lighted her face; she half turned away. "You need money for carfare tonight? I could give you a dollar."

"Yes, I'll need it."

Skip wouldn't be there tonight, he was in Las Vegas. Eddie was to meet Karen and see what news she had, whether she'd gotten a chance to inspect Stolz's room and count up any of the money.

At eight o'clock Eddie was in the hall outside the typing room, waiting for the break. When Karen came out he gave her a shy smile, not quite sure how to act toward her in Skip's absence. She was Skip's girl. He wanted to be friendly, not in any way fresh. She seemed young and to Eddie terribly inexperienced. "Hello."

She looked at him blankly and started off. They went down to the end of the hall where the big double doors stood open to the terrace and the outside stairs. Lights bloomed here and there, illuminating shrubbery and paths. She turned on the terrace to face him. For the first time Eddie noticed her manner, how tight with strain she seemed, how excited.

She put a hand on his arm. "I saw it."

For a moment he failed to understand. Then he remembered. "You found the money?"

"There's too much of it! I couldn't begin to count it. I'm scared. I'm afraid Skip won't leave it alone." She trembled; her hand quivered on Eddie's arm. "It's tied up in paper bands, stacks and stacks, and somehow it's not like real money at all."

Some of her keyed-up mood communicated itself to Eddie. "It's really there." He moistened his lips with his tongue, staring off into the dark.

"You'll have to explain to Skip—it's too big. There's too much of it, and taking even a little would be dangerous."

"How could I tell him?" Eddie said reasonably. "He'd say I was crazy. Don't you know anything about him? Don't you see the way he is?"

She gazed at him as if trying to understand what he wanted to tell her. "It's not like real money at all," she said, wanting to make that point. "There's too much, it's just like paper. Like green, printed paper."

He shook his head, feeling sorry for her. "It'll seem real enough to Skip."

She wanted to draw back and didn't know how. She wanted to get Skip's mind off the money and still keep him interested in her. She was scared because she had told Skip about what was hidden in the Havermann house, and now nothing on earth could stop this thing from happening that was going to happen.

The wind touched her dark hair, blowing it in feathery streaks across her face. Her eyes were young and frightened. Eddie tried to find words to comfort her, but it was too late. It had been too late the first time she had opened her mouth to Skip about that money.

CHAPTER SIX

At seven o'clock Skip stepped off the bus at the depot in downtown L.A. He felt stiff, tired, and gritty. He went into the coffee shop adjoining and had a cup of coffee, sitting hunched over it, his mind a blank. His only desire was to get home and have about eight hours' sleep. Then he'd gas up the jalopp and run over to see Eddie.

He passed Mr. Chilworth's big house and walked through the overgrown yard to the rooms above the garage. He looked around, in case his uncle was about, but saw nobody. He went up the stairs, the zipper bag swinging from his fingers, and opened the door. Uncle Willy was there and so was someone else, a big old man with a pale freckled face and a great shock of gray hair. Skip said, "Uh. Hello." He tossed the zipper bag to his bed.

"Sit down, Skip. We want to talk." His uncle nodded toward the other man. "This is Tom Ranigan. Big Tom to his friends."

"Hiya," said Skip. He sat down and pulled off his shoes and scratched the back of his neck.

"How did you do in Las Vegas?"

Skip's head jerked up. He fixed his gaze on Big Tom. "Hey," he said.

"That's right. Big Tom knows all about it."

"Well, I'll be damned. Cook me for crowbait," said Skip incredulously.

"It's this way, Skip. You and Eddie are a couple of inexperienced young punks. You've got hold of something here, maybe. Maybe not. If it's real and there are possibilities in it you're going to find yourselves with a wildcat's tail in your mitt."

"Now let's get this all straight," Skip said between his teeth. "You've brought in this old gazoo to run things?"

"Now don't speak disrespectfully of Big Tom," Willy advised. "He's a man with a great reputation. Earned it hisself, I might add."

Skip was staring evilly at Willy. "I oughta bust you in the snoot. Tipping my plans to some broken-down has-been. What is it, really? You figuring on a cut for yourself?"

"Don't get excited."

Skip was full of a cold rage. He went on to describe in detail just what he should do to Willy, and what Willy could do with Big Tom. The two older men listened for a short while in silence; Willy in a warning stillness and Big Tom biting his lips. Then Big Tom said, "This isn't getting us anywhere."

"You'd better listen to us," Willy warned. Skip went on with the bitter tirade, and Big Tom stood up on his chair and all at once there was a gun in his hand. It was a shining and well-kept-looking Luger, not new but quite businesslike. Big Tom walked over to Skip, and Skip's words died in his throat.

"It's like this, kid." Big Tom whipped the gun against Skip's face, not edgewise but cupped flat in his hand. The skin burst in a few places and Skip spun sidewise, catching himself at the rim of the bed. He felt as if the bones of his jaw and of his face in front of his ear had snapped to splinters. He sucked a breath in agony. He saw Big Tom through a whipping red haze. "Now that wasn't anything," Big Tom said, "but just a tap. I can do better if I have to, lots better. I like bouncing punks around. If you weren't Willy's kin I'd show you how I like to do it."

Skip pushed erect and touched his face with a shaking hand, not sure there was anything but pulp there. His head still rang from the blow, the blow that hadn't looked like anything when he'd seen it coming. It occurred to him that this man called Big Tom had a freakish strength and power in his hands.

There was something else here, too, something that frightened Skip more than the blow. The old man exuded a terrific authority. He was boss, kingfish, top banana, and he knew it. Skip tried to feel his way past that bulwark of power, and couldn't. There was no softness, no pity. The old man stood over Skip with the Luger balanced in his palm and he had Skip under control as he would have controlled a puppy.

Skip crouched, rubbing his aching head, and stared across the room at Uncle Willy. Willy looked back with a sort of mild sympathy, as if he was sorry that Big Tom had

had to do what he had done. Skip tried to figure out where his uncle had located this character so quickly, and came to the conclusion that Willy must still have some connections with his old organization. He had dug Big Tom out of his past, and now the job was being taken away from Skip and given over to this old con. Skip thought he would have pegged Tom for an old con even in passing him on the street.

Willy said mildly, "Now straighten up, Skip, and listen to reason."

Skip said nothing. Words boiled in his mind, but he knew what he would get in return if he spoke them.

"He'll be all right now," said Big Tom, putting the gun back into his belt at his belly. "He just needed a little lesson."

The ringing was leaving Skip's ears. The pain remained at the side of his skull. He looked from Willy to Big Tom and thought, *There's going to be a way to pay this back.*

Big Tom sat down again. "I want to talk to you about this Eddie Barrett." He waited, as if he might expect some remark from Skip. "I want to know what he expects out of this thing."

"Money," said Skip gratingly.

"Don't get sassy with me," Big Tom warned. "I mean, what're his plans? What's he want to do afterwards?"

Skip blinked, then lowered his eyes. He knew that some importance attached to his answer. He wished he knew in what way so that he could reply in a way to screw things up. Everything he could do now, short of outright rebellion, he meant to throw in their way.

Finally he thought, It's too soon. I don't know enough yet. He said, "Eddie's mother is sick. He wants to help her, pay for a doctor or something. The old man drinks and raises hell. Eddie wants to get away from him. At least, that's what he talks about."

"What does he want for himself? Clothes? A car?"

"Yeah, a car."

"Does he have a girl?"

"Not that I know of."

Big Tom sat in silence, as if digesting this information. Willy said, "Tell us about Las Vegas, now. What did you find out?"

"Stolz is over there. He's a partner at the Solano Sea."

Willy nodded. "One of the big ones. Well established. You saw plenty of play in the casino, I bet."

Skip said, "Yeah, it looked okay."

Willy moistened his lips. "The next step, the girl. You've got to make sure this Karen knows where the money is, how much it is, how long before Stolz might get back. When will you see her? Not before tonight?"

"I'll see her in class."

Big Tom said, "We want to ease this Eddie Barrett out of it. Can you handle it?"

"I don't know. Suppose I can't?"

"It would be better for him if you do it," Big Tom said.

"He's going to be surprised," Skip said. "I don't know how he'll take it."

"This is the way he'd better take it. He'll forget he knows Karen or ever heard of the money. He'll think you changed your mind."

Eddie might believe he'd changed his mind, Skip thought. He might even want to believe it. Eddie wasn't nearly as keen on the job as Skip was. But Skip made a mental note: he wouldn't follow any directions in regard to Eddie. Eddie might turn out to be what Skip needed. He could be the one to foul them up, if Skip could plan it. "Oh, he'll go along," Skip said to Big Tom. "I'll convince him it wasn't a good idea, there wasn't any money there after all, or something like that."

Big Tom said, "You let us know exactly what he says, how he takes it."

"Sure. Sure."

"There are going to be two other men in this. You won't meet them," Big Tom continued. "I'm just telling you about them so you'll understand about the split. We're letting you in for ten per cent."

Skip said nothing. His rage was already throttled down; if anything, this lessened it. He saw with a cold certainty how Willy had rooked him, conned and betrayed him. Willy had taken the great golden opportunity, the once-in-a-lifetime chance, and turned it over to his friends. For what?

As if Willy knew what he was thinking, he said, "That's what I get too, Skip. Between us—twenty per cent. Twenty per cent of possibly a million. Nothing to do, just sit tight." He leaned forward as if trying to rouse some hint of enthu- siasm from Skip. Or perhaps an uneasy warning stirred in him, the knowledge of what Skip was like when he was frustrated or crossed.

Skip didn't look at his uncle. He said to Big Tom, "Are you cutting Karen out, too? She gives you the information and you leave her there with nothing, leave her for the old woman and the cops? Karen's kind of young. She's liable to squawk. She'll squawk about me. For ten per cent, I'm the pigeon?"

"You don't have to be," said Big Tom easily. "You can handle her the way you do Eddie Barrett. Tell her it's all off, you've changed your mind. Or if you want, take her away somewhere when the job comes off." He made an emphasizing gesture, lifting a hand, the thick fingers curled above the fleshy palm. Skip noted the broad and powerful wrist. "There's this, though. When she leaves they'll look for her. They find her, they've got you then. They'll work on your alibi. It had better be a good one."

"In the can on drunk and disorderly is best," said Willy.

"I'm not crazy about it," Big Tom argued. "Still, they can't blink away a jail booking."

Skip got the complete picture now. He was going to be paid off to keep out of it, to build an unassailable alibi in case he was picked up. Willy would be paid for information given. The girl and Eddie were to be brushed aside as expendable. They would have no knowledge of Big Tom, represented no danger, had nothing with which to trade. The hog's share of the loot would go to Big Tom and his two faceless helpers; plus, Skip suspected, something put aside for the organization.

"Why won't you use me on the job so I could rate a bigger cut?" Skip begged, testing them.

Big Tom nodded in judicious approval. "In anything smaller I'd do just that. For Willy's sake. But, kid, I've got experienced men I've worked with before. I know just how good they are and, even more, that in an emergency they won't lose their heads and goof off. They'll never break where the bulls are concerned, either. They've been tested." His eyes mocked Skip with a wolfish humor.

"Skip," said Uncle Willy, as if making a last plea for understanding, "it's not just the job. It's the beef, the squawk afterwards. Things can go haywire in a hell of a hurry. Somebody's singing your name to the wrong folks before you even know it. Now just picture it, because I know you never did, but try: you and Karen and Eddie with all that dough. What were you going to do afterwards?"

Skip didn't answer. He had nothing at all to say to Willy. He looked at Big Tom politely and said, "If you don't mind, I'd like to get some sleep now. I've been up all night and I'm beat."

"Sure. Get your sleep." Big Tom stood up and nodded to Uncle Willy and they went out and down the steps to the yard. Skip gave them a couple of minutes. Then he rose and, walking silently in his socks, he went into the bathroom and inspected his face in the mirror. An area of bruised flesh was swelling and darkening in front of his ear. He turned sidewise, inspecting it, and curses growled in his throat. He ran cold water into a towel, squeezed it lightly, patted the swollen place. It was going to look like hell tonight; and in class, under the bright lights, he'd feel like a fool. He decided then not to attend class but to wait for Karen outside on the break.

He went back to the bed and lay down on top of the covers and stared at the ceiling. The picture was clear, but his own part in it was not.

Uncle Willy and Big Tom went out to the alley, where Tom's Ford sedan was parked. An old lime tree was blooming against the fence and the air was sweet with the smell of its blossoms. Willy said, "He'll be okay. He got a little excited there at first, but that was natural. He's settled down now."

Big Tom said slowly, "When you get a chance, talk to him. He has a chance here he'll never get again."

Willy nodded excitedly. "Sure. Nothing to do. A wad of dough just for sitting still. What more could he ask?"

"Keep an eye on him," Big Tom said. "I'll be back tonight around eleven."

"We'll be waiting for you." Uncle Willy turned and hurried through the yard to the rear door of the big house at the front of the lot. In the kitchen was Mr. Chilworth in pajamas and robe; he'd already had breakfast and Uncle Willy was surprised to find him here. Mr. Chilworth was staring nearsightedly into one of the kitchen drawers.

"What is it, Mr. Chilworth?"

"Oh, there you are!" Mr. Chilworth opened a second drawer. "I need a screw driver. One of the pulls on my dresser drawer is loose."

"I'll fix it, Mr. Chilworth."

"Would you? That's fine." He was near the back windows now; through the screened porch the stairs of the room above the garage were plainly visible. For a moment Uncle Willy worried whether Mr. Chilworth might have seen him with Big Tom, an item Big Tom wouldn't have liked; but then he reminded himself of Mr. Chilworth's extremely bad sight. There was nothing to be worried about.

Mrs. Havermann walked along the upstairs hall to the stair railing. From above she could see the lower hall, wide and shadowy, and through an open archway a part of the parlor. She leaned on the railing and stood still for a moment as if listening, then called, "Karen! Karen, are you down there?"

In Stolz's room Karen was on her knees before the open door of the old-fashioned wardrobe. She had a hand stretched to touch the heap of money inside. Her expression was one of fascinated fright. When she heard Mrs. Havermann's voice she jerked her hand back as if from something hot. Quickly she got to her feet, shut the walnut panel, and walked across the room. She brushed at her face, then glanced at the sweat on her fingers in surprise. She opened the door just a crack.

"Karen!"

She was safe. From upstairs Mrs. Havermann couldn't see the door of Stolz's room. Karen came out, stumbled a dozen feet, looked up.

"Oh. There you are. Come up here, Karen, I've something to show you." Mrs. Havermann indicated some linens over her arm. As Karen mounted the stairs she moved away from the railing to meet her. "I've been looking into the hall closets. Here are some sheets nearly worn through. We'll cut them up for pillowcases and dish towels. The nice thing about a sheet . . . when it wears, there's so much left to do things with."

Karen came up the last of the stairs. Her heart still thumped and she couldn't keep her breathing steady. As she took the linens from Mrs. Havermann she expected some comment, some notice—surely Mrs. Havermann would see her excitement. But as Karen ventured to lift her eyes, she found Mrs. Havermann's gaze focused just beyond her. The look in Mrs. Havermann's eyes was as always vaguely pleasant and cheerful.

In that instant it occurred to Karen that through the years Mrs. Havermann had always regarded her like this. As if she were a shadow through which Mrs. Havermann must peer. As if she were not quite a living being. As if there lay between them a vast distance, an ocean of indifference.

Karen saw this now because in her fright she expected the attention of the other woman.

Mrs. Havermann transferred the sheets to Karen's arm and then said unexpectedly, "Were you in the kitchen just now?"

Karen, caught off guard, could only stammer, "No, I wasn't."

Through the rimless glasses Mrs. Havermann's gaze seemed mildly puzzled. "I have the strangest impression lately that you drop out of sight now and then. Just disappear. You aren't hiding kittens in the cellar again, are you?" The tone was not exactly chiding, nor was there much curiosity in Mrs. Havermann's attitude.

Struck with guilt, her tongue thick, Karen got out, "No, I'm not."

There was no argument, no real interest on Mrs. Havermann's part. She was picking at the sheets. "Measure the towels by those in the kitchen. Be sure to get them square. Don't forget to change the bobbin on the machine. Black's on it now." She smiled vaguely and turned away. She was short and stout and heavily corseted. The artificial tightness of the corset lengthened her torso, flattened the softness around her middle. She walked as though encased in a barrel whose contents must be kept in delicate balance. Her gray hair she piled high on her head in an effort to gain height.

Mrs. Havermann had stood near, had looked at her and had turned away, and to Karen it was at once a miracle and a revelation. She had never quite realized before how indefinite and withdrawn Mrs. Havermann's manner was toward her. Along with gratitude over her escape from discovery Karen felt almost a sense of shock that Mrs. Havermann had paid so little real attention.

Karen went back downstairs. Past Stolz's room—she gave it a quick guilty glance—and then on to where the hall made a right-angle turn in the direction of the pantry, the huge kitchen, and the rear entry. In the sewing room, once a maid's room, stood a long cutting table made of boards laid on a pair of sawhorses. Karen put the sheets here, got scissors from the sewing machine, and set to work. She had no objection to the task at hand. She was not lazy, and the solitude of working alone gave her time to think.

The thing on which her thoughts fastened most desperately was the great store of money in Stolz's room. It at once fascinated and repelled her. Most of all, from it she absorbed a stunning sense of danger.

She had worked for a short time when she heard Mrs. Havermann's quick step in the hall. The door opened and the older woman stared in at her. There was no vagueness now; behind the rimless glasses Mrs. Havermann's eyes were sharp. "Karen, have you been in Mr. Stolz's room today?"

On the heels of fright, the denial was automatic. "I never go in there."

Mrs. Havermann hesitated in the doorway, her excitement subsiding. "Well, it's rather odd. There's something out of place in there. I can't remember seeing it earlier." She tapped the door lintel with a nail, obviously puzzled.

Karen's heart filled with fear. She knew exactly what must be out of place in that room; Stolz's overcoat was lying on the bed. Stolz kept it folded on top of the money so that in first opening the wardrobe you didn't see the heap of bills. When she had gone in to stare in fascination at the treasure she'd put the coat on the bed, and when Mrs. Havermann had called her she'd forgotten to replace it.

"Perhaps Mr. Stolz changed things around," she managed to get out.

"It's not the furniture." Mrs. Havermann turned back into the hall. "I wonder . . . could he have laid it out for the cleaners and I not noticed?"

Karen waited. Concerning Stolz, Mrs. Havermann was closemouthed, inclined to sentimental secrecy; Karen decided that she would not be told all about the coat. "Didn't he send suits out when he was here?"

"No, that was time before last." Mrs. Havermann nodded, as if deciding for herself what to do with the coat. "That's it—he wants it sent off to be cleaned."

Karen was at a loss, though she saw the pitfall she had constructed for herself. When Stolz returned there would be conversation about the coat, where it had been found and what had been done with it; and whether she was able to argue Skip out of what he wanted to do, or not, she was in trouble up to her neck.

She looked mutely after Mrs. Havermann. She needed help, needed to confide; but Mrs. Havermann was already too far away.

CHAPTER SEVEN

Karen walked out to the terrace when class was dismissed for the mid-evening break, and she was startled to find Skip there waiting, smoking a cigarette, grinning at her. He pulled her close and kissed her, and something in Karen, constricted and repressed, born of her life at Mrs. Havermann's, seemed to burst and flood her with warmth. She returned the kiss hungrily, clutching the shoulders of his jacket. Then she lay against him, grateful; here was someone to whom she could confide the disaster with the coat. She told Skip about it all in a rush.

Skip listened, at first with indifference. He'd heard already from Eddie of Karen's reaction to the money, her frightened excitement about it. It took a moment to realize that this wasn't more of the same, the reaction of an inexperienced girl, but that a bad break had really occurred. Then it struck him with irony that this would be exactly what was needed if he meant to string along with Big Tom and Uncle Willy. Now was the time to pretend everything was off, that he was afraid Stolz would be warned and have the money guarded. But even as he opened his mouth to speak Skip changed his mind. He noticed that Karen was looking at him closely in the dim light.

"What happened to your face?"

His hand jumped automatically to touch the sore spot. "I . . . auh . . . I fell, getting off the bus in Vegas."

"It looks terrible! You should have a bandage on it."

"No, it's okay."

She lifted a hand gently but he brushed it aside.

"How much money does Stolz keep there?"

"I don't know."

"You haven't counted it? What's the matter? Scared or something?"

"It scares me," Karen admitted, wide-eyed. "There's so much of it. Too much to count." She touched his arm timidly. "Leave it alone, Skip."

He flipped the cigarette into the dark. "Big bills?"

"All I saw were hundreds."

Skip rubbed his hair, stretched lazily. "Sounds as if Eddie and I ought to do it tonight."

Her eyes were stark. "Why . . . how could you?"

"The way we planned. You let us in around midnight, keep an eye out for the old woman, keep the dog quiet. How long will it take? Not over a couple of minutes. It'll be a breeze."

"It won't turn out the way you think. I know it." She stood in the direct light from the door, trying to make Skip look at her; but now his gaze had a vagueness that reminded her of Mrs. Havermann's. He peered beyond her at the hall, and she blurted: "What will happen when Stolz gets back?"

"To you? Nothing. You could lie your way out of it. Or

come to me." He reached for her, pulled her close again; he could feel her heart thumping like a rabbit's, and the knowledge of her fright and torment filled him with amusement. "What about the old lady? You ever tell her my name, mention seeing me in school?"

"I guess she knows I talk to you. I've told her things you've said."

"Chrissakes, that was a dumb thing to do. Now she'll have a line on me."

"No. Rather than have anyone suspect you, I'll stay and make up a story; someone's been prowling around when I got home at night, and I saw them. I'll describe somebody. A stranger."

Skip stood musing, wondering if Karen were capable of carrying it off. Then he wanted to laugh at himself. Of course Karen wouldn't be able to stand up to the characters Stolz would bring in. They'd have her babbling the whole thing in a couple of minutes. He let his mind dwell on some possible methods they might use, grinned, shook his head, while she watched. "You wouldn't back down? Even to Stolz?"

He was just having fun though she didn't know it. "I'd never give you away. Never." She put her arms around him, tucked her head against his shoulder. The warning bell rang in the hall, signaling the end of the break.

"You know old lady Havermann could come to class, check up on whoever you've been seen with."

Karen gave a troubled sigh.

Again, Skip thought, the opportunity presented itself. Say now to her that you're calling it off, go out and build a rock-solid alibi, take the ten per cent from Big Tom and keep your lip buttoned. But again perversity, or perhaps the memory of the gun in Big Tom's fist, kept him from speaking. He was even beginning to enjoy himself, the opportunities offered and shrugged off because, as Uncle Willy would say, he was just a punk and didn't know better.

"I'm just a damned punk," he said aloud, amused with it.

"No, you're not. I love you."

Abruptly he shook her arms free. "Now what the hell kind of talk is that?"

"Well, it slipped out. But I do."

"Listen, Karen. You cut it out. There's not going to be any crap like that here, not between us."

"Sure, Skip."

"Come out this way when class is over. I'll be waiting for you."

She turned away. The wind brushed at her short dark hair, tumbling it; she held it off her face, glancing back at Skip. At the door she blew him a small, light kiss from her fingers.

What a sap she was, Skip thought.

At eleven o'clock Big Tom went into the bath of Uncle Willy's room above the garage, drew a glass of water, stepped to the open door to drink it. "He's always here by eleven?"

"Has been, up to now. Even earlier sometimes." Uncle Willy sat on his small bed with a garden-seed catalogue in his hands. Mr. Chilworth had expressed a fantastic but determined whim for snapdragons and phlox. He wanted them along the side of the house and along the front walks. It was crazy, an abominable amount of work for Uncle Willy. "Class runs to ten, seven o'clock to ten. He ought to of been here by now."

"Why in hell doesn't he go to school daytimes?"

"Well . . . Skip's an adult. Adult classes are almost all at night. You know, most people work."

Big Tom frowned. "He's staying out later for some reason. I smell something funny."

Uncle Willy said soothingly, "Oh, Skip wouldn't try anything."

"He'd better not. I don't want any preliminary fooling around, a job I handle. There's been too much already." Big Tom put the glass back into its holder above the small basin, came back, sat down on Skip's bed.

As if to get Big Tom's attention off Skip, Uncle Willy asked, "You got somebody in Las Vegas already?"

"Benny Busick. He flew over, going to look around and see if Stolz has had a tax beef in the last few years."

"If Stolz has—it'll be tax dough?"

"Probably not. It's the ones the tax bulls haven't looked at who still feel like hanging onto their little nest eggs."

"I'll bet Stolz is robbing the tax bulls blind," Uncle Willy decided with a grudging touch of admiration.

Big Tom leaned his arms on his knees, rubbed his chin, frowned at the open light in the middle of the ceiling. "I don't know. There's something screwy about the setup, a chunk like that left unlocked and unguarded in a house with an old woman and a girl. It's careless-like, and a boy such as Stolz isn't careless, ever. It's almost like he's got some kind of guarantee. Something to keep everybody away."

"There's a dog," Uncle Willy offered.

"Oh, hell, I'm not talking about a dog."

"Maybe he's keeping it for a friend."

Big Tom smiled slightly, as if Uncle Willy had cracked a joke.

They wasted forty-five minutes in the hamburger joint and afterward let Karen out at the corner where the bus stopped. "Now we'll go on to the vacant place and circle around through those trees," Skip told her. She was standing under the glow of a street light and staring across the wide lawn at the house. The house was dark except for a small bulb burning in the enormous cavern of the porch.

"Did you hear me, for Chrissakes?"

"Sure. Sure I heard you."

"The back door. We'll be at the back door."

"What about afterwards?"

"Stay and size it up for a day or two. If she gets wise the money's gone and starts to get hold of Stolz, or makes a squawk for the cops, run. Don't bother to pack a bag or any of that kind of crap. Just walk off."

"Where? Where should I walk, Skip?"

"I'll figure a place. Get going."

Eddie was alone in the car with Skip now. As the car labored up the grade to the rising ground and the trees, Eddie said, "I felt sorry for her there."

"For what? We'll be doing her a favor, getting her out of the dump. The old woman works her tail off, and look

84

at the clothes the chick wears. Not a goddamn thing you wouldn't put on your old maid aunt. She wears cotton underpants, for Chrissakes!"

"She told you?"

Then Eddie knew that Skip was laughing at him, and he shut up. The car labored up the rise and drew to a stop beside the dark curb. Eddie got out. He heard Skip shut the door on the opposite side, not slamming it, ticking the lock quietly. "I wonder why we've never seen a patrol car through here," Eddie said. "Big homes and all. You'd think they'd keep an eye on things."

"They've got an eye on you right now, friend," Skip jeered. "They're reading your mind with a goofus machine. Wait'll we get to the back door. They'll jump out of the bushes."

"Ah, shut up," Eddie said mildly.

It seemed easier this time; they were familiar with the ground and the extent of the grove of trees. They came to a point where they could see the dark bulk of the house, a dim light in one of its upper windows, a little window like a bathroom's; and all at once Eddie was struck by the panic, the aversion and fright he had felt before. His feet grew leaden, his palms sweated. A cloying tightness shut off his breath.

"What's the matter with you?" Skip had paused; by starshine Eddie could see him looking back.

"I . . . Just a minute." He sucked in a deep breath and tried to force himself to relax, tried to force the freezing scare out of his mind. He tried to blank out all thought, since the panic seemed rooted in thinking. But through his mind poured memories of other times, things that he and Skip had done. Most of the jobs had come off all right. They'd sneaked tires and junk off wrecking lots, lanterns and fusees and tools out of freight yards, even cigarettes, a whole huge carton of them, from a half-plundered freight car on a siding. They'd stuck up old man Fedderson's candy shop . . . twice. Stockings over their heads, cap pistols. It had been fun. For God's sake, why did he have to feel like this now?

Was it because of the times things hadn't turned out okay? Like when he rolled the bum in the alley, a dead-end passage behind a garage and a bar and a warehouse, and the patrol car had turned in on him with its lights blazing?

Or the time Skip had whistled from the back yard, the killdeer call, and he'd gone and Skip had been white and sweating. Skip had borrowed a couple of bucks and had walked to the corner and had been picked up right there, still within sight of the house. Later that day Eddie found out that Skip had been caught robbing a market storeroom of a case of whiskey.

Was it the failures that drained him now of strength?

Skip was standing still, a little way off. "What are you doing there? Are you . . . For Chrissakes, are you getting ready to chicken out on me?"

Eddie's stumbling answer died in his throat.

Skip took a lithe step toward him. "If you are, goddammit, get on with it. Faint. Or drop dead. Or start running. Don't just stand there with your legs locked together. Why in hell should I care what you do? I can't think why I needed you in the first place."

"You said . . . if something went wrong—"

"It is. It is," Skip said wryly. "You're punking out just like Unc said you would."

Eddie failed to catch the revelation at the moment; he was too busy with his own miseries. But the harshness of Skip's tone had the usual effect; it dried up his terror. There was more to be feared from Skip's contempt than from the mysteries of the old house in the dark below them. "Oh, God," Eddie said, "there for a minute . . . I don't know. It just hit me."

"What are you going to do now?"

"I'll be okay. Let's go."

"Sure." Skip stepped closer still and his fist shot out. The blow to Eddie's midsection was small and sharp, and it hurt. Eddie grabbed his stomach; his tongue curled out over his teeth; breath whistled in his nostrils. "Now," Skip said. "Now we'll go."

Eddie stumbled after him. Karen was down there, outside the back door; Eddie could make out that she'd taken off her coat and shoes. She padded toward them. "Be quiet! She's in bed but I heard her turning over; I don't think she's asleep."

Skip was looking up at the house. "Where?"

"The corner there upstairs."

"Open windows?"

"No. She's scared of the night air. Leaves the bathroom window open, the light on in there. I don't know why, maybe because she's nervous."

"What the hell are we beating our gums for out here? Let's go in," Skip said.

"I don't dare turn on a light," Karen whispered. "You'll have to follow me. Don't fall over anything."

"Just lead me to the dough," Skip said. "I won't make any racket."

They crept into the house. This was a windowed porch. Eddie could see the shining white enamel ledges of laundry trays, a black door open in a white wall; he smelled disinfectant and soap.

"This is the washroom," Karen whispered. "We'll go through the kitchen and on to the hall. There's a big table in the middle of the kitchen, pots stacked on a shelf underneath. For God's sake don't touch that table."

"Where's Stolz's room?"

"I'll have to show you."

Feeling his way in the dark, Eddie saw with incredulous wonder how stupid they had been. He and Skip should have known all about the house, every obstacle; should have managed to look it over during the old woman's absence, or drawn a map from Karen's description. Now they had to be led along as if blind; and above him he felt the old woman on her bed, wide awake and waiting to hear them stumble. He fought panic again, glad that Skip couldn't see.

They got through the kitchen. Eddie's eyes were adjusted to the dark; he could see the white rectangle of the table's surface, so there was no problem in avoiding it. He kept expecting to bump into something invisible, though. Or to kick some pan or dish left for the dog to eat or drink from.

Where was the dog?

He wanted to ask Karen, but she was ahead of Skip and his voice might carry, might rouse the old woman upstairs.

The hall was darker, closed in and stuffy. The house was old; you could smell age in it, old varnish and dead wax and underpinnings touched with mold, all clean and swept on the surface. There was none of the familiar effluvium of home, where the choking goiter and a palpitating heart kept his mother all but bedridden, and flies and dirt grew thicker day by day. Eddie's shoes brushed the carpet, roused no smell of dust, just that of old wool and mothproofing. He all but ran into Skip. Skip and Karen had paused before a door.

"Where's the dog?" Eddie got out.

"Upstairs. I shut him in my room."

Skip said, "What the hell's the matter with the door?"

"It doesn't open!"

"Here, let me try it." Skip moved; Eddie heard his soft dry step on the wood beyond the carpet; he heard a sort of grunt and a faint click of metal. "For Chrissakes, it's locked!"

"No, it couldn't be!" Karen whispered in a positive way.

"Well, it goddamn well is. Here, Eddie, have a go at it and see if it isn't locked."

Eddie tried the knob, warm from Karen and Skip's hands. "Sure it's locked." He said in Karen's direction, "Maybe she's always locked it at night and you didn't know it."

"It's never been locked before," Karen said positively. Her voice was beginning to quiver.

"What about the windows?" Skip asked.

"You'd need a ladder."

"Well, for Chrissakes get me a ladder!" Skip was angry and he was losing control, forgetting to keep his voice low. Eddie expected at any moment to be bathed in light, to find the old woman standing and looking at them from the other end of the hall.

"The ladder's in the garage. I'll have to get the garage key from the hook in the kitchen."

After agonizing minutes of creeping back through the dark house, of delay while Karen put on her shoes and got the garage key and opened the garage and found the ladder, of the risk of noise and exposure, of Skip's climbing the high old wall of the house above the basement windows, it came out—

The windows of Stolz's room were locked as tight as its door.

CHAPTER EIGHT

Eddie carried the ladder back to the garage and Karen, moving beside him in the dark, showed him where to stow it away. They came outside again and found Skip. He stood without moving, utterly silent, and Eddie had a sudden sense of warning. The next moment Skip had turned on Karen. He grabbed her and slammed her into the wall and then jerked his hand back and hit her with the edge of his fist. Her head snapped and Eddie heard the bump it gave against the garage wall. "You goddamn bitch!"

Eddie said, "Skip, cut it out. We can't have a racket here."

Skip paid no attention. "I'll show you!" He snatched at her hair, got his fingers into it, jerked her forward almost off balance. She tried to catch his knees to keep from falling; he slapped her hands away. She'd begun to whimper. She stumbled around Skip, off balance, and then he yanked her head up again and she gave a small shrill cry.

Eddie moved then. His action was involuntary, without plan. He put out a foot and then with a quick tentative step he was closer and pushing Skip in the face with his open hand. Skip tried to hang onto the girl and handle Eddie, but he couldn't do it. Eddie got a good leverage under his chin and jabbed hard and Skip fell over backward. He was on his feet again in an instant, like a dropped cat. He moved in with a flurry of blows.

Eddie wasn't Skip's kind of fighter. Skip danced and flicked his fists and tormented an opponent, while Eddie just stood and took punishment and waited; but pretty soon Eddie found what he was looking for and he let loose a solid heavy blow that snapped Skip's head back and flung him off his feet. He sat there under the starshine, not hopping up as before, but stunned, groggy. "You leave her alone," Eddie said. "From now on."

There seemed an eternity of quiet out there in the dim dark beside the old garage. Eddie stood over Skip. He was tensed, a hot fiddle-string tautness filling him, his fists hard as hammers. He was ready for Skip to move. Skip sat bent, his head hanging. His light-colored hair shone a little in the gloom, but his face was in shadow, and Eddie couldn't even guess what sort of expression was on it. One thing he knew, Skip didn't accept defeat. His reaction was always simply to be meaner and tougher and cleverer than ever.

Oddly enough, Skip didn't say much. He got to his feet, grunted, brushed at his clothes, and then looked around as if for Karen.

Karen was across the open space, near the house. The light from the little window high in the wall shone down on her, and Eddie could see the look of shock she had, the tear shine on her face and the frightened attitude of her body. When Skip walked toward her she backed to the wall.

Skip stood, balancing on the balls of his feet, his hands

in his pockets. He said almost indifferently, "You're okay, aren't you?"

Eddie wondered why she didn't run into the house. She was scared; Skip's violence had astounded her. But he heard her whisper, "Yes, I'm okay."

"Sore at me?"

"You didn't have to hurt me," Karen said. "Finding the door locked was just as big a surprise to me as it was to you." She was looking at Skip now as if something about him was new and unfamiliar.

Skip stood quietly, almost meekly. It was an act, of course. Eddie had seen Skip do it a thousand times, and though it was false, a fantastic pretense, he could almost believe–as Karen must–that Skip was sorry for what he had done. "Well, sure, I blew my stack over nothing. Why do you think she locked the door if she's never done it before?"

"On account of the coat," Karen said wearily. "Mr. Stolz kept it lying on the money, covering the money so you didn't see it if you accidentally opened the door of the wardrobe. Maybe she knew where the coat belonged or maybe she didn't recognize it because Mr. Stolz never wears it. I don't know. She got excited when she found it lying on the bed."

After a while Skip said musingly, "What a rotten break."

Karen didn't say anything. She knew that Skip blamed her.

Skip said, "Well, you'll have to find that key tomorrow."

"Oh no, Skip! Please! It's too dangerous. It's time to stop now."

"You'll find it," Skip insisted. He didn't take any step

nearer, but something in his eyes that Karen could see, that Eddie couldn't see from where he stood, seemed to frighten her. "You'll be sure that door's not locked tomorrow night, and we'll be here right on schedule. Then afterwards we'll have fun."

Eddie wished there was some way he might have comforted her. She looked as if her world were coming apart at the seams.

Eddie let himself into the rear of the house. There was no one in the living room tonight. From the bedroom he heard his father's snoring. He knew that his mother must be lying in there awake and miserable, trying to rest because that was what the doctor had told her to do, but kept from sleeping by the grunts and snorts of her husband.

The bastard abused her even in sleep, Eddie thought, tiptoeing across to his own door. Inside, he pulled off his jacket and shirt and flung them over a chair and sat down on the bed to unlace his shoes. They were tennis sneakers and quite shabby; the laces had knots in them and Eddie had to pluck with his nails until they loosened enough for him to shuck off the shoes.

The money in Stolz's room would buy a hell of a lot of shoes. A million other things besides, too. Eddie threw the tennis sneakers under the chair and sat thinking of what he would buy with his share of the loot when they pulled off the job. There would be a tremendous amount of cash. Enough for dozens of suits, shirts, sharp new shoes, a car. An operation for his mother, removing the ugly balloon at the base of her throat. Clothes for her, all kinds of silk dresses, a fur coat, new furniture for the house if she wanted it. And all this, dazzling as it was, would only scratch the surface.

An odd uneasiness stirred in his mind.

It was hard to conceive of all the possibilities wrapped up in the bundle of money in Stolz's wardrobe. When you were used to a dollar or two, even a hundred seemed more than you could count. A thousand was fabulous. With five thousand you'd feel like doing something silly, maybe, just to be spending, something crazy like buying a gold-plated switch blade . . . or taking dancing lessons so you could do fancy steps better than anybody . . . or buying all silk shirts with monograms . . . His imagination sought for other images, roamed in a dazzle of overwhelming splendor.

Under the dazzle the uneasiness increased. Eddie put his finger on it. The natural, crazy things you did with a lot of money were the things he and Skip had to be careful not to do.

They needed a plan. He hunted around through the cloud of dissatisfaction and apprehension in his mind and decided that what worried him was Skip's apparently deliberate lack of planning. Skip was either unable or unwilling to choose a course of action and stick to it. He wanted to improvise, to make his decisions when the time came for them; and even Eddie could see the danger in it.

Eddie roused himself, shed his pants, snapped off the light, and crawled under the thin covers. He stretched his body on the bed. To hell with worrying. This job was Skip's baby. Let Skip do the worrying.

He found himself thinking of Karen then. The idea came abruptly; she was too young for Skip. The clothes the old woman put on her made her look old for her years; but inside, Karen was terribly unadult. It was as if she'd been stunted at about the age of twelve, never allowed to grow further, so that in addition to the youngness there was an inner hunger and craving, a need. The need had sent her to Skip, as if he might show her how to grow up and be a woman.

You got smart around Skip, Eddie thought, but you didn't grow up because Skip has never grown up and has no idea how to show anyone else to do it.

Eddie sat up in the dark, rubbing his head. The memory of the moment came back, how he'd stood over Skip with his fists knotted, wanting Skip to get up and dance around him some more so that he could land another scorcher.

Now why did I want to do that? Eddie wondered. Why in Chrissakes should I get so worked up over Karen, when she's Skip's girl and he ought to be able to treat her the way he wants to?

Skip was twenty-two. My God, he ought to know by now how women should be treated.

Skip stood in the dark at the foot of the steps to Willy's room. He smoked a cigarette, listened to the voices from upstairs. That big bastard was there again with his uncle and Skip had an ominous feeling that his coming in late was a mistake.

Finally he went on upstairs and opened the door. Uncle Willy sat on his cot in his pajamas and cotton robe. His

skinny feet, the toes knobbed with corns, were tucked
Buddha-fashion at his knees. He smiled nervously at Skip.
"Well. Hello. You're pretty late tonight. Something keep
you?"

Skip knew all at once that his clothes and his face
showed the effects of his bout with Eddie. "I had a fight
over a bitch."

"Now that's interesting. Who's the lady?"

"Karen Miller." Skip hadn't moved away from the door.
He was waiting for some action from Big Tom, who was
standing across the room. The big brush of gray hair
caught the light; the freckles were brilliant against the pale
skin. A typical con, Skip thought in disgust. He thought
he'd never seen a guy who showed prison like Tom did.

Big Tom began to walk toward him on the balls of his
feet. He exuded authority and power. He could run over
Skip or anybody like a hippo over a mouse. Skip hated him
so fiercely it was dizzying.

Big Tom stopped about two feet from Skip. "Who'd you
fight?"

"Eddie Barrett."

"That half-Mex punk?" Uncle Willy cried. "You still
messing around with him?"

"Tell us about it," Big Tom suggested.

The tone warned Skip. He had to take this easy. He said,
"Well, this girl, this Karen Miller, she's trying to make a
play for me. She wouldn't talk about the money unless I
took her home in the car. Eddie came along."

"You went out to the house?" Big Tom asked sharply.

"Not all the way. I got her to the neighborhood, near

enough to walk, and I asked about the dough, Stolz's
money, and she got cute. I was . . . uh . . . urging her
a little when Eddie blew up. Oh, hell, in the end it wasn't
anything. But it took time." Skip thought, Time's what I've
got to explain. That's all they give a damn about.

"Eddie got sore over what you were doing to the girl?"
Big Tom asked. "That doesn't sound so good."

"Ah, he's soft in the head. I'm glad now I'm not going
through with it with him."

Big Tom was watching him sharply. "You explained
about that?"

"Oh, sure, once Karen had spilled, I let on I'd turned cold
on the idea."

"How did Barrett take it?"

"Just . . . nothing." Skip shrugged. "He didn't have any
complaints. Hell, he wouldn't know what to do with a saw-
buck if he got that much together."

"He heard everything Karen had to say?"

"Yeah, I couldn't get rid of him." Skip was feeling his way
cautiously, wary for any sign of violence from Big Tom, any
indication Big Tom needed to prove who was boss again.
"He's just a sap, he doesn't know what it's all about. He's
busy thinking all the time about his mother being sick and
his old man steamed up on vino."

Big Tom seemed to believe Skip. He walked over and sat
down on one of the battered straight chairs, a discard from
Mr. Chilworth's place up front, reversing the chair and
folding his big arms across the back. "I want to know about
the place. The house, inside. The money. Where it is and
how much."

"Well . . . as for the house . . ." Skip sat down on his bed. "The way Karen describes it, there's a hall from the kitchen. Several doors in it. Stolz's room is to the right. He keeps the money in a wardrobe, a kind of thing Karen says is half drawers and half a kind of cupboard for clothes."

"I know about wardrobes."

"Well, the money is in the big half under a coat, just piled there. She hasn't counted it. Looks like a lot."

"The room's never locked?"

"Nah, it's never locked." Skip forced himself to meet Big Tom's gaze with an air of frankness. *It'll be locked when you get there, you bastard. There won't be anything inside, though.*

"That's what I don't like. The carelessness." Big Tom was frowning. Uncle Willy picked up a flower-seed catalogue off the cot and riffled its pages nervously. "If it was anyone but Stolz . . . If it was the old woman, for instance. I could believe she'd stuff the money in there and be stupid enough to think no one would find it. Hell, they do it all the time, little old ladies keeping a wad in a teapot or a tomato can."

Skip shook his head. "The money belongs to Stolz. Karen's sure of it."

He had a flash of hope that Big Tom would worry himself right out of the job, but the hope faded. Big Tom got up and picked up his coat, shrugged into it. "Well, there's a reason, God knows what. I don't expect to move, though, until I hear from Benny in Las Vegas. That should be tomorrow. I'll get in touch with you, Willy. You and Skip can be figuring out where you'll be. I happened to think— Skip being in class, that would be good enough. You need to be where people will see you, Willy; I don't believe I'd do the jail routine."

"You can't argue with a jail record," Uncle Willy repeated.

"It makes you look bad," Big Tom said firmly. "Do something else."

"All right."

"I'll see that Snope is notified; he'll be standing by in case we need him." Big Tom went to the door, paused there to give Skip a studying glance. "I don't think we'll have any trouble. Getting it shouldn't amount to much. Keeping out of Stolz's way afterwards might take a little work. Or it could be he can't afford a squawk and there's nothing to be afraid of."

And I handed it over to you by blabbing to Uncle Willy, Skip thought, his expressionless eyes on Big Tom's face.

Big Tom went out quietly, closing the door. His steps went down softly on the stairs to the yard. A minute later they heard his Ford start up in the alley. Uncle Willy said, "It's going to work out fine, Skip. You'll see, we'll have a fat cut, no work or effort, nothing pinned on us by the bulls."

"Just as you say." Skip stood up and began to undress. In his shorts he went into the bathroom, washed his teeth, scrubbed his face and hands and arms with soap. He looked at his face in the mirror above the basin. There was no doubt but that he and Uncle Willy bore a strong resemblance to each other. To Skip, however, Willy was hideous with the wasting of time, of frustration, poverty, and denial. It was the way Skip would look after years of small jobs and petty thefts and jail. Damned if I will, Skip told himself. There's this one big chance and it's got to be for me.

Tomorrow night Big Tom and his friends would move in on old lady Havermann. He and Eddie had to be there first. There was this one break; he didn't have to account for himself to Tom; he was supposed to be in class. Tom had been a sap to trust him, but everybody makes mistakes. Tom must have made plenty or he wouldn't have that old burned-out look of a con.

He went back into the other room. Uncle Willy was in bed, the covers pulled up around his skinny shoulders, facing the wall.

"Turn out the light. Good night, Skip."

"Night."

Skip clipped off the light and lay down. Just before dropping off to sleep he thought briefly of Karen as he had seen her last, standing in the faint glow from the little window high in the old woman's house. She'd looked scared to death. Eager, too, eager to be sure that Skip wasn't really mad at her, that lashing out at her had been the impulse of a moment. Skip thought drowsily, I can do anything I want to with her. I can beat her half to death and she'll come crawling back, wearing that same sappy look, wanting to be sure I'm not really mad at her. Why are dames like that? Why don't they, for Chrissakes, have any guts?

Skip smiled to himself in superior humor and then drifted off to sleep.

Big Tom was awakened by the clamor of the phone in the other room. It was still dark. The dry canyon wind blew in at the open window. A couple of cats on the bed near his feet lifted their heads as he stirred and reached for the rubber sandals.

He snapped on the little lamp and looked at the clock. A quarter of four. "What the hell . . ." The phone was ringing like a fire alarm in the quiet of the lonely house. Big Tom padded into the front room and lifted the receiver. "Yeah?"

"Benny Busick here."

"Huh. You calling from Vegas?"

"That's right. Look . . . uh, this transaction we were discussing. There's something here I can't put my finger on. Working at it. You didn't need that information for a day or so, now, did you?"

"Today, you crumb. I need it right now. What in hell are you doing over there?"

"Don't blow your goddamned stack at me. I'm just telling you. It's an angle. I'm working on it and I need time."

"By noon today or don't bother."

"Okay, I'm still trying. Take my advice. Lay off until you hear from me." Benny's gravelly voice was wheedling.

"It's noon or nothing." Big Tom put the telephone back in its cradle and sat there yawning and rubbing the mane of gray hair off his forehead. Three of the cats who had been sleeping on chairs awoke and looked around as if it might be time for breakfast.

Big Tom scratched and yawned himself fully awake and then took stock of the conversation just concluded. Hell, there had been no reason for him to snap Benny off like that. Just because he'd been irritable from interrupted sleep and Benny hadn't seemed to have anything definite except a request that Big Tom wait.

That was it, he decided. Benny's desire for a delay, a need for time to search and listen—that had roused the sudden anger.

For a moment Big Tom felt a sense of shock, and then he wanted to laugh at himself. Here he'd been so convinced that there'd never be another job in his life, just this little dump of a house and the plants and the cats—and all the time the hungry impatience had been building in him, the determination to have one more big one.

He was shaking his head over it as he went back to bed, snapped off the light and lay down. The moment of insight passed quickly from his mind, leaving only the crystallized decision to have Stolz's money at the first opportunity.

CHAPTER NINE

Mrs. Havermann never got out of bed much before nine. She usually came downstairs around nine-thirty, always completely dressed and with her hair combed and pinned high and with a touch of powder on her cheeks. She always paused in the lower hall to look over yesterday's bouquet on the table there and to make up her mind what she wanted in the vase today. Then, if the mail had come, she inspected that. There was ordinarily very little—ads addressed to Householder, or perhaps a few bills.

After her husband had died Mrs. Havermann had dropped almost all of her social contacts and had gradually taken on the habits of a recluse. This came about from choice, though not consciously so. It was a matter of a weathered ship finding haven in a peaceful pond. She had been married for many years to a demanding and autocratic man. He had loved social functions and had had many friends. When he wasn't hard at work in his contracting business he played with equal gusto at being a host, gourmet, horse bettor, traveler, or yachtsman. The pace had been stormy.

Though she had never admitted it to herself, her

sensations on hearing of her husband's death in a plane accident had been mostly of relief.

The withdrawal from social participation had been accompanied by an emotional withering. She no longer wanted to be involved with other people; she wanted peace. She protected herself, unconsciously, by the pleasant air of vagueness, by concentration upon household trivia, and by a mild daydreaming about Stolz. The fact that he was much too young and too sophisticated to return that interest was also, indirectly, another part of her defense. There was no real danger that the daydreams might become reality and burst the emotional vacuum in which she lived.

Mrs. Havermann had no comprehension of how her futile and barren situation affected Karen. She considered herself as acting properly in the capacity of mother to the girl. There were food, shelter, and clothing, a training at a trade as well. Behind her wish for Karen to become a nurse had been the unrealized idea that if in the future she should become ill or bedridden Karen could care for her properly. The thought of Karen serving her in her helplessness involved nothing more emotionally moving than that Karen would thus be repaying her for the years of keep.

Karen had refused to go into nursing school. In reproof, Mrs. Havermann had declined to finance a course at business school, had instead made the girl study commercial subjects in adult classes.

On the morning following Skip's and Eddie's abortive attempt to enter Stolz's room, Mrs. Havermann came downstairs at twenty-five minutes past nine. She picked over the flowers on the hall table and then examined the three letters which Karen had brought in. The first was a dental bill, the second a notice of a sale on some hosiery at a department store where she kept an account. The third letter, also an ad, caught her instant attention. It was the notice of the opening of a new local office by a locksmith.

The incident of the coat being out of place had focused her thoughts on Stolz's room, and now the coincidental arrival of this ad had for her an odd, superstitious impact. She turned and stared at the door of Stolz's room, just visible in the corner where the hall turned. She tucked the locksmith's ad back into the envelope, and then, wearing a thoughtful look, she went out to the kitchen.

Karen was at the kitchen table with classwork spread out before her. Mrs. Havermann glanced at her briefly, then looked quickly around the room. Karen's eyes seemed red and swollen. Mrs. Havermann wondered momentarily if Karen could be coming down with a cold. "Well, it's a nice bright day," Mrs. Havermann said, going to the kitchen range. There was coffee hot in the percolator and Mrs. Havermann poured herself a cup of it. "What would you like for breakfast today, Karen?"

"Whatever you'd like, Aunt Maude." Karen was gathering up her books and papers. Her manner was dull and depressed. She put the books into a locker and took dishes and silver from another cupboard.

The exchange was so routine that Mrs. Havermann would have been astonished had Karen actually offered a preference in food. She carried her cup of coffee to a window and stood there to drink it while looking out at the sky. The sun bathed the yard in bright morning light.

Frowning, Mrs. Havermann noticed that the lawn between the house and garage had a trampled appearance, and this annoyed and puzzled her. She sipped at the coffee and thought about it. She didn't speak of her impression to Karen but decided to go out after breakfast and look more closely at the area. Suddenly she thought again of the locksmith's notice and an odd alarm ran through her.

When the coffee was gone she set the cup on the table, went to the refrigerator, took out a bowl of leftover cereal, two small eggs, and a package of bacon. At the stove she reheated the oatmeal, boiled the eggs, fried two slices of bacon.

Karen was abnormally listless and untalkative, and her obvious depression penetrated even Mrs. Havermann's aloofness. But Mrs. Havermann at once dismissed it from her mind; she wanted to think about the trampled grass and other household matters. Biting into her breakfast toast, she said, "I'm going into town today."

Karen showed a trace of curiosity. "Downtown?"

"Not into downtown L.A. It's just too far. I have an errand a few blocks from here. The shopping center."

Karen nodded indifferently. Her unhappy melancholy was so obvious that for once Mrs. Havermann almost reversed her attitude of cheerful inattention, almost asked Karen what was wrong. But habit was ingrained. Instead she urged on the girl a second cup of coffee.

She would not have dreamed of explaining to Karen that she was thinking of putting a new lock on Stolz's door. As it was now, the door was fastened by the primitive apparatus installed when the house was built—fifty years, she thought, if it was a day. She'd had a terrible time locating a key for it. For her own peace of mind, best to reinforce it with something new.

Her secrecy in regard to Stolz had had its origins in the breakup of his marriage to her daughter Margaret. Margaret, just out of school, had met and been attracted to the older, worldly man, and when the mother had met him she too had been charmed. The marriage had been brief, though ironically friendly. Margaret had met another man and Stolz had amiably stepped aside. Mrs. Havermann's attitude had been incredulous. Compared to her own difficult, tempestuous marriage, Margaret's had been ideal. She disliked the new son-in-law. She felt a deep disappointment over what she considered Margaret's foolishness.

All this had happened a little over nine years ago, when her husband had brought Karen into their home. It had been the natural thing not to explain the involved situation to a child. Afterward, especially since Havermann's death, the habit of secrecy had become a part of her withdrawal from normal communication. Stolz remained on friendly terms, visiting frequently, and now he was almost the only person besides Karen and the gardener whom Mrs. Havermann saw much of. Her mildly sentimental daydreams about him she kept entirely to herself.

The hints she had dropped to Karen, that Stolz might have money here, had been the result of a moment's desire to brag, to let someone else see how much Stolz trusted her. Perhaps, too, to convince herself he might be as interested in her as she was in him.

When they had finished breakfast Karen cleared away

the table and washed the dishes and the stove. Mrs. Havermann went into the front of the house and looked around. She had not forgotten her idea of giving the back yard a close inspection. She wanted to figure out a way to have Karen away from the rear of the house.

She could not quite pin down why she didn't want Karen watching when she went outdoors. Certainly she felt no distrust of the girl.

Mrs. Havermann thought, Karen might think me a fool if she saw me out there staring at the ground. This summed it up for her, though there was something more she didn't try to analyze.

She returned to the kitchen shortly. Karen was sweeping a few crumbs from the floor around the table. Mrs. Havermann said, "That reminds me, dear, I think the front hall could use the dust mop this morning. The wax is there; it just needs a good buffing. Use a little pressure."

"Yes, Aunt Maude. What about flowers?"

"Well, the ones Mr. Dooley picked yesterday still look pretty fresh. Daisies and lupines wear well." Mrs. Havermann went out into the service porch. "I'll be sorting laundry while you do the hall."

Karen went out of the kitchen, and Mrs. Havermann heard her at the mop and broom closet in the pantry. When the sound of Karen's steps had quite died out Mrs. Havermann went quickly into the back yard. She walked around inspecting the grass, which somehow upon close view didn't show the disorder she had noted from a distance. It was hard to see any definite markings; the old tough growth of Bermuda lawn grew every which way,

with patches here and there devastated by moths or by in-
adequate watering. She made up her mind to speak to Mr.
Dooley. He had charged her last week for insecticide and
manure, and heaven knew the water bill was big enough.
There should be a luxurious green carpet here.

She went over and glanced in at the small side door of
the garage. It was dim inside and smelled musty. Her old-
fashioned Packard limousine sat on its blocks. She never
used it any more. The car hadn't even had a license renewal
for the past two years. Probably the tires were rotted, she
thought, looking at the dust on them.

She went back into the yard, and some feeling which
another person would have identified as a hunch took her
over toward the windows in Stolz's room. Old Mr. Dooley
had turned the earth here, wet it deeply, and scattered
zinnia seeds. The bed was in an excellent state to retain
impressions, and Mrs. Havermann could see quite clearly
the twin marks made by the feet of the ladder and a man's
shoeprint. The shoeprint was that of a ribbed rubber sole
such as a tennis shoe.

She felt frozen, locked in panic, hanging there over the
marks in the earth while the blood pounded in her throat
and temples. Her hands turned cold. Her knees shook.
This was nightmare.

After a moment she hurried back to the garage, went inside, and snapped on the light. The ladder sat in its usual
spot. No, not quite. Mr. Dooley had used the hose yesterday, and now one of the feet of the ladder was placed on
a stray end of the hose, squeezing it flat. The ladder must
have been moved since Mr. Dooley had put the hose in the

garage. Had Dooley himself used the ladder? She was certain he had not. Nor would he have left it like this, possibly to damage the plastic hose by its pressure.

Mrs. Havermann knelt down and rubbed shaking fingers around the bottom of the ladder and some crumbs of earth came off. She rubbed the crumbs to powder between her fingertips, and the earth still held a trace of moisture, as it would if it had come from the wetted bed of zinnia seed.

Someone had used the ladder to gain entry to Stolz's room. Had they succeeded? She rushed a second time to the zinnia bed and looked upward. What she could see reassured her. There was no indication that the sills had been prized, and she could see the locks in place on the crosspieces.

She felt a little calmer. Someone had tried to get in, but they hadn't risked a forced entry. Sneak thief, she thought. She looked at the footprint in the earth and a sly, menacing figure seemed to build itself in the air above it. Mrs. Havermann shuddered, averting her eyes as from a living criminal, and then she went quickly back to the laundry room.

I can't just go to pieces, she thought. I must go at this sensibly. She stood by the white enamel tubs and forced herself to consider, to think the situation through. The best and most obvious course was to go to the police and report an attempted burglary.

Would Stolz want her to do this? Somehow she thought not. She remembered vividly the scene in the library more than two years past—she and Stolz sharing a brandy, the room warmly lit, Stolz's darkly handsome face looking at her over the brandy snifter, and his voice: "I'm going to ask a favor. Don't be afraid to turn me down, Maude. I'd like to keep a bit of money here."

She'd said promptly, a little coquettishly, "Well, why shouldn't you?"

"Would it make you nervous?"

"I keep money in the house, Dan."

"This might be much more than what you're accustomed to having around. If I leave it here, shall it be our secret, yours and mine? I don't have to warn you about careless talk."

"I wasn't born yesterday." She had smiled at him, inwardly delighted. Not only at his trusting her so far but, as well, that the storing of money in her home made a kind of tie between them and a guarantee of his continuing visits.

"If anyone ever tries to question you——" A touch of sharpness in his glance; she noted it.

"I'd tell them nothing, never fear."

His emphasis on caution and secrecy had impressed her. True, she had hinted about the money to Karen, but she quickly dismissed the memory. She was positive that Karen had too much honor and good sense to go babbling about it to outsiders.

She again thought of Stolz's words: ". . . shall it be our secret, just yours and mine?"

He wouldn't want her to call the police and explain about the money, she decided. At least, not yet.

The first thing to do, if she was to pursue a sensible course, was to check and make sure the money was still there. Though she had dropped hints to Karen, on her own part Mrs. Havermann had maintained a curious sense of honor; she had felt that Stolz wouldn't want her spying on his hoard and so she had given in to her curiosity only once, some six months after he had requested permission to leave the money here; and at that time she had found over fourteen thousand dollars in one of his wardrobe drawers.

Now, composing herself in case she met Karen in the hallway, she went upstairs to her room. The key was in her bureau under a box of handkerchiefs. As she took it out, she heard Karen in the bathroom adjoining. "Karen?"

"I'm washing the tile. I didn't get finished yesterday."

"That's good." The bathroom faced the rear yard, overlooking the area between the house and the garage. Had Karen looked out of the window a few minutes before, she would have seen Mrs. Havermann below, but Mrs. Havermann had shut the frosted pane tight upon arising, as usual; there was no reason for Karen to have opened it. The girl hadn't seen anything.

These ideas trailed through Mrs. Havermann's mind as she stood there with the key in her fingers, and something more followed. She always kept the bathroom light burning at night. She'd read somewhere long ago that such a light was one most apt to keep off burglars, seeming to indicate that one was up out of bed either using the toilet or taking medicines—in either case relieving a condition which had made one wakeful. Now it occurred to her that the bathroom light being on during the night had been what had kept the burglar from making a forced and perhaps not entirely silent entry. He had thought that someone was awake upstairs.

She nodded to herself, pleased in spite of her worries that her small precaution had paid off. She went downstairs, unlocked the door to Stolz's room, went in, relocked the door, and looked around. She had been here only yesterday, checking to see if she should dust; her eyes flew at once to the coat on Stolz's bed.

She had almost convinced herself, since first finding it, that the coat had actually been on the bed all of the time since Stolz's departure and that she had somehow overlooked it. But now a new conviction startled her. Someone had already been in the room, searching for the money.

Puzzled over this, as well as sure that her conclusion was the right one, Mrs. Havermann opened the drawer where she had once seen and counted the fourteen thousand dollars. To her surprise there was no money here now, only some of Stolz's shirts and underwear. She opened other drawers in the wardrobe, and then looked into a set of drawers built into the closet. Such drawers as did not hold clothing were empty.

He's taken the money away, she thought vaguely, aware that her sensations were a mixture of relief and disappointment. The next instant she became illogically convinced that the thief had been successful, the money stolen! In fright she finished her search by throwing open the door of the wardrobe compartment designed to hang clothes. At sight of the enormous heap of green packets she stood transfixed, and as she comprehended the size of the heap and the amount of money which must be here, she gave a shrill cry and almost fell to her knees.

She was as stunned as if she had come upon some monstrous growth which in stealth and darkness had increased beyond all bounds. While she stood tottering a couple of packets slid off to the floor, and she jerked her foot away as from a poisonous and malignant fungus.

She managed finally to slam the wardrobe door, then went to the bed and sat down groggily. Fear seemed to have congealed in her marrow. Under the poleaxed numbness some thoughts fluttered: one, that there must be something illegal in Stolz's hiding such a vast amount; and also, a brief feeling of outrage that he had chosen to put it here. In that instant she nearly grasped how illusory was the sentimental dream she'd built up around him.

She rose from the bed and, without another glance at the wardrobe, went into the hall and locked the door.

She passed Karen on the stairs. Karen carried cleaning materials in her hands, had her eyes fixed where she must step. For a moment Mrs. Havermann paused. Her emotions had been stirred as they had not been in years. She was on the verge of panic and the need to talk to someone was almost overpowering. She blurted, "Karen!" and the girl looked at her.

Like an electric spark there seemed to flow between them a blaze of sympathy and compassion. There was in both a terrible need to communicate. Mrs. Havermann's stark eyes and chalky skin brought out in Karen the yearning to console, to listen and reassure. And for the first time in Mrs. Havermann's life she felt the girl there as a living human being on whom she could depend, whose love she had earned and deserved.

Mrs. Havermann put out a hand, opened her lips to speak. In the next moment she would have spilled her panic and confusion, and Karen would have confessed all of Skip's plans.

But the words wouldn't come. In the years of repression, of rejection, the loving and confiding words had withered and died. Now there was only awkward silence, the ticking away of the moments as she and Karen faced each other on the stairs.

Mrs. Havermann licked her lips. The warm turmoil was dying in her, and Karen seemed to be receding to a more proper perspective. She tried to think of something to say. "I'll be going soon," she got out.

Karen waited as if still not giving up hope, her face full of the ache to be accepted. But Mrs. Havermann brushed by her and went on up the stairs.

CHAPTER TEN

"When Mrs. Havermann came out of the front door, wearing her hat and coat and carrying a purse, she found the big collie lying on the porch. His fur was golden in the sun. He lifted his head and wagged his tail, blinking his eyes against the light. She stopped abruptly to stare at him. Where had he been during the night? She hadn't heard a bark out of him, though his little house was just beyond the garage.

He greeted everyone, she knew, with a happy frisking, often too exuberant to be welcome. But surely, if a stranger had gone so far as to put a ladder on the wall, he'd have at least barked a little. The dog's silence became a part of the menacing and incomprehensible whole, like the misplacement of the coat on Stolz's bed and the thief's directness in going straight to Stolz's window and no other.

She hurried down the front walk, then down the paved street to the main boulevard where the bus passed. A cab happened to come by before the bus did, and she took that. She got out at the shopping center.

The locksmith had a small office in a corner of one of the supermarkets. There was a counter, beyond it a desk and a table full of tools, shelves of stock, and some key-cutting equipment. The man who came forward when she stopped was about thirty, very clean-looking in a smart gray apron. "Yes, ma'am."

She had taken his mailed notice from her bag. "I received this today."

"One of our ads. What can I do for you?" He was sizing her up and perhaps he saw the fear she tried to repress, for his glance sharpened with interest.

"I wish to have a lock installed. Locks, rather. A door and two windows."

"Yes, ma'am. Any particular make or type in mind?" He was pulling a scratch pad and a pencil toward him on the counter.

"The best. The very strongest. You choose them."

"We have some remarkable new locks for windows now," he said pleasantly. "Absolutely burglar-proof. What's the address, please?"

She gave the address of the tall old house, and he wrote it down. She stammered then, "There is another thing I want to mention. I don't care to have anyone come to the house in a . . . any kind of truck with a sign on it. That is, if anyone happened to be . . . to be around outside . . ." She stumbled to a halt, her face alternately blanched and crimson. He was looking at her directly now, a stare of open curiosity.

"It's not an outer door?"

"No. A bedroom."

"You prefer that we come in a private automobile?"

"Yes, please."

"What about our satchel of tools? The boxes of locks?"

She saw gratefully that he had quickly grasped her need of secrecy. "Could you disguise them somehow? If I were to buy some groceries—"

He thought it over for a moment, tapping his teeth with the pencil. He had the air, she thought, of entering into a game. Could it be, she wondered briefly, that he considered that he was humoring a crocked old lady? "I have even a better idea. Now, you just don't want to advertise that you're bringing in a locksmith, is that it?"

She nodded mutely.

"Well, what about a plumber?"

She looked blankly into his friendly gaze, not understanding.

"I know of a plumber's truck I could borrow. Has the plumber's sign on it."

"Why, that would be fine!"

"How about tomorrow morning?"

For an instant she didn't grasp it, and then she felt the blood drain from her skin. "Oh, but this must be done today!" She had a moment's horrifying image of herself lying awake tonight listening for the thief.

"I'm not sure that I can borrow the truck today, the other truck. Besides, you see, I have a partner in this business. He's out now on a commercial job and won't be back till late. I could hardly leave the office for such a length of time."

She was desperate. "Ten dollars extra if you'll come today!"

He nodded. "For ten dollars I'll come right this minute."

"No. There's someone that I . . . Could you make it at one o'clock?" A plan had come spinning into her head from nowhere. Karen loved the big downtown stores. She'd pretend she hadn't found what she wanted here and send Karen downtown for the afternoon to look for it. Something inexpensive and hard to find, some certain brand of wax or polish. But no. In Karen's unusual mood she might become discouraged too quickly. Here Mrs. Havermann, recalling that moment on the stairs, had a twinge of guilt. Best to give the girl something to look for that she'd find interesting, some folderol thing. Cosmetics. Or clothes. Or perfume. That was it, some kind of cologne they didn't make any more. Keep her running to perfume counters, a pleasant chore.

This all ran through her head with the speed of light; the man behind the counter must have seen how she had cheered up.

"One o'clock on the nose," he said in a friendly manner.

She felt better now, enough to wonder what he thought of her behavior. "I guess you don't get many requests like mine," she said with a small effort to be cheerful.

"More than you'd think, ma'am." He smiled in a reassuring manner.

She went back outdoors. The sunlight seemed garish, almost scalding. She saw a cab pull into the parking lot, raised her hand in a signal. An old friend and neighbor got out, old Mrs. Potts, and she had to stop and commiserate over the woes of arthritis and colitis. Once in the cab and headed for home, a confused panic almost overwhelmed her. She was aware of her aimless, bumbling behavior. Perhaps she was, after all, doing the wrong thing. Surely the logical action would be to call Stolz in Las Vegas.

She could pretend she hadn't investigated his room, hadn't seen the money, was merely worried over indications of attempted entry.

She could ignore the emphatic request, repeated since the time he had begun staying overnight, that she never try to contact him in Nevada. A silly rule. Obviously he didn't want anyone over there knowing of his private retreat in her house—but suppose a fire or other catastrophe had wiped out his money? Wouldn't he want to know? She rapped on the glass panel between herself and the driver.

"Yes, ma'am?"

"Stop at the first public telephone."

He nodded, braked, swung toward a drugstore on a corner.

Inside it was cool and dim. The druggist, in a white jacket, was squatted before an array of rubber beach toys, building a pyramid. He rose and looked at her. "The phone," she said.

Then she saw it, the black box inside its cubbyhole at the rear. It seemed to promise relief from intolerable anxiety and tension. She went into the phone booth and drew the door shut after her.

Stolz, however, was not at the Solano Sea. She had to leave a message for him, to be delivered if and when he came in.

Big Tom was sitting in a chair by the telephone, his expression glowering when the call came at eleven forty-five from Benny Busick.

"Benny here."

"Yeah. Yeah."

"Take it easy, now, for God sakes. Keep the lid on."

Big Tom hitched himself closer to the phone. "Look, crumb, why aren't you on the way back here? I need you outside tonight. I've got things to tell you."

"Not me, you don't. No, sir, I don't want any part of it."

"What do you mean?" Big Tom felt like biting the phone. "You don't want what we lined up—you crazy?"

"I don't think you know *what* you've got lined up." Benny's tone had grown high and squeaky with defiance.

"Spill, crumb."

"Look. This . . . this information you got. It's known here in Las Vegas, and the ones who know aren't doing a damned thing about it. Lay off, Tom. Don't touch it."

"You must have a screw loose," Big Tom growled into the phone.

"Maybe I have. I got a nose, too. This deal smells funny."

"Now you lay it on the line or, by God, when we meet again I'll stomp you flat." The words were bitten off crisply, and Big Tom knew the effect they'd have on Benny in Las Vegas. Benny's narrow face would be wet with sweat and his chest would be heaving. He'd be staring into the phone like a wild-eyed tomcat.

"I'll . . . I'll call you when I've got something," Benny said in an almost inaudible voice. "Stick around." To Big

Tom's disgust, the wire went dead. Benny Busick had hung up.

Big Tom slammed the receiver into its cradle. For a moment he remained in the chair, staring at the opposite wall. Then, with a hard angry look on his face, he went out to the kitchen. He stood by the drainboard and drummed his nails on the tile, looking out of doors through the window over the sink.

When his anger had subsided somewhat he went to the kitchen range, heated a cup of coffee left in the pot, drank it standing in the middle of the floor. A couple of cats had roused themselves from a midday nap and now came looking for lunch. Big Tom grumbled at them, meanwhile spooning processed fish into their bowl.

He went back to the living room, sat down, dialed a number on the phone. It rang twice before someone lifted the instrument at the opposite end of the wire. "Yeah? Hello?"

"Ranigan here."

"Oh. Hey, wait a minute, will you?" The voice turned from the phone and spoke to someone else. "Doll . . . run down t' the corner and get me some smokes, huh? Couple a cartons."

A girl's voice whined a complaint, dim in the distance.

"Be a good kid, huh? Filter tips, king size. The kind like it says on the TV, not a burp in a bellyful."

The girl's voice rose sharply in sarcasm. "Oh, Harry, you're killing me!"

"Don't forget t' bring matches, two, three them little packs."

She grouched: "Oh, okay, I'm going."

Dimly Big Tom heard a door close behind her. Harry said, "She's a good little twist; I just don't want t' explain everything t' her."

"Same one you had last year?" Big Tom said evenly.

"You mean Eva? Ah, she ran off with a bum, played the cornet in a dive, him and her are over t' Phoenix now."

"Well, I wouldn't confide in this one either. She might not last any longer than the others."

"Who's confiding? I never confided the time of day t' none a them." Harry sniffled into the phone. "Business is business and dolls is dolls. That's my motto!"

Big Tom dropped it. "Busick just called."

"Yeah, what's he say now?"

"More of the same. Lay off, it don't smell right. He's got butterflies in his underpants."

"Well, what you going t' do?" Harry asked uncertainly.

"I'm going to pull it. To hell with him." He waited, and Harry said nothing. "I don't see what could be wrong."

"Well, like you said yourself, it's funny that it's laying there where it is and nothing guarding it."

"I've made up my mind to get it and take a look at it," Big Tom said. "Then if there's something queero we can have a bonfire. I wanted Busick outside just in case, but he won't come back now."

"Ah, we can do it ourselves, you and me," Harry said with renewed confidence. "It'll be a snap."

"You know what to bring," Big Tom told him. "Be here by ten."

"Sure, I'll be there."

Big Tom put the phone into its cradle. The look of anger and disgust had smoothed from his face. He went out into the small kitchen again and found three newcomers mewing into the fish bowl. He fed them, then went out the rear door to the yard. Shaded by a big pepper tree, this area was cool and breezy. He walked the narrow bricked path back to the lath house. Before stepping inside he looked around carefully.

He watered the potted fuchsias and the ferns. He had another look outside. Then he went into a corner of the lath house and lifted a flat stone set into the creeping green moss. Below the stone was a small compartment lined with brick. From among other things Big Tom selected a plastic-wrapped object which had, in spite of the wrappings, the unmistakable shape of the Luger.

Carrying the wrapped gun, he went back into the house. He stood for a minute in his small front room, listening to the silence of the canyon. Then he sat down, unwrapped the Luger and inspected it thoroughly, meanwhile whistling through his teeth.

Skip went into the bathroom and examined his face. What Eddie had done looked like a mere scratch; the damage wrought by Big Tom darkened the whole side of his face. Skip washed and dried himself, brushed his teeth. He'd slept later than usual. Well, that was all right. He'd be up later tonight, too. He looked at himself again in the mirror, and the thought of Big Tom brought flickering lights into his eyes.

He went back to the outer room, dressed, went downstairs, and crossed the yard to the big house. Uncle Willy was in the outer porch on his hands and knees, wielding a scrub brush. A pail of soapy water stood by him. "Watch it," he yelped at Skip. "It's all wet in here. Go around to the side door. Watch that kitchen. Where it's still damp, I don't want it all tracked up."

"Give me fifty cents, I'll get something down at the corner."

"Fifty cents, hell. I'll be through here in a minute. Ten minutes, it'll be dry as a bone here. Those eats in the kitchen are free, Skip. Don't forget that. Don't try to fifty-cent me when there are free eats for the cooking."

Skip moved a little closer. "You ought to try to start getting used to having dough, Unc. Now handing out fifty cents would be a good beginning. Practicing, you could say." Uncle Willy was shooting poisonous looks at him and jerking his head toward the inner recesses of the house where Mr. Chilworth might be listening.

"You weren't worried about him hearing you talk about his free eats," Skip pointed out reasonably. "What's wrong now? Chrissakes, he's got it bugged out here or something?"

Uncle Willy propped himself on his heels. A thin lock of gray hair had fallen over his eyes. "Skip, you try me. You really do. If you weren't my own sister's boy, I swear I'd kick your butt in."

"Want to try?" But Skip went around to the side door and let himself into the pantry, walked on to the kitchen, and looked around for something to eat. Willy scrubbed his way to the rear door. He propped the mop there, dumped the water on the shrubbery, and came to the side door and was soon in the kitchen with Skip. By now Skip was frying three eggs in about an equal quantity of butter.

Willy heated the coffee, poured two cups full.

"Oh, God, that damned business of working on your hands and knees always did get my back to aching. I bet I washed ten thousand miles of corridor when I was inside. It just wore my spine out. I can't hardly stand to get down like that any more."

Skip flipped the eggs around to get them thoroughly covered by the butter. "You won't have to work like this much longer. You'll be flying high."

Uncle Willy frowned at him across the cup. "Are you nuts? I'm not going to make a move for a year. What I learned, I learned the hard way, but I got a few things that stuck with me and one is—one important one is—you flash it, they nab you. You want a collar, just start living high and throwing it around." His voice was low, little more than a whisper. "And that's my word to you, Skip. Look poor and talk poor and ride poor. A Cadillac will get you the jug as sure as the sun rises."

"Yeah, yeah." Skip took a plate out of the cupboard, dumped the eggs on it, took bread from the toaster and buttered it. He ate standing up at the sink as usual. "Suppose the law never hears about it? Suppose Stolz can't afford to let on what's happened?"

"That'll be even worse," Uncle Willy whispered. "That chance, that Stolz is hiding tax dough, is what made me take the job away from you and give it to Big Tom. Big Tom can protect himself. If the heat's too bad he'll make a deal.

He'll sell it back to Stolz himself, for a cut, of course. Now how would you and Eddie ever have handled that?"

"You talk like Stolz is the bugger-man," Skip jeered, but a memory jumped into his mind: the big man with granite fists who had stood outside Mr. Salvatorre's door in the Solano Sea.

The man with the granite fists was one of Stolz's little helpers. He could crush you like a marshmallow with one wallop. Under the repose, the cumbersome politeness, lay a well of savagery. You saw it in his cold and measuring stare.

Skip looked at Uncle Willy; a nervous smile flitted across his face. Willy didn't see. He was staring into his coffee.

"What are you going to use for an alibi?" Skip wondered.

CHAPTER ELEVEN

At six-thirty Uncle Willy was dressed in a blue suit, a pale blue shirt, red bow tie; and his black shoes shone like Mr. Chilworth's front windows. Skip, too, had on the outfit he usually wore to go out, slacks and the leather jacket. He had scrubbed, his hair was combed neatly, and a faint dusting of talcum subdued the bruise along his jaw. Uncle Willy came out of the bathroom drying his hands. He was smiling foxily. "I've really got a good one this time."

"You really have," Skip agreed. "Who's this bird who's going to pick you up?"

"Name of Mitchell, he said over the phone. The meeting's out on West Larchmont. My God," Uncle Willy said wonderingly, "just think! I'll be sitting in a meeting of Alcoholics Anonymous telling the folks my drinking problems when Big Tom is pulling that job."

"It's a real good alibi," Skip agreed again. Privately he was surprised that Uncle Willy had thought up so original an idea.

"You know," Uncle Willy went on, his tone warming, "at first when Big Tom nixed the idea of being in the can, I thought of going to a bar, talking to somebody there, making an acquaintance. But then I thought, hell, the bastard would be drinking and, with my luck, he wouldn't be able to pick me out of a line of midgets when the time came. So then I thought, What's the opposite of a goddamn bar? And the answer came, Why—Alcoholics Anonymous." He beamed at Skip in pride. "I figured it out all by myself."

True, Skip thought. Everybody at the A.A. meeting would be interested, observant, and sober. You couldn't ask for a better batch of witnesses. "It's okay," he said.

Uncle Willy brushed some lint off his pants with a flick of the damp towel. "I'll be hard put to keep from laughing, though. I'll be thinking to myself of all that dough I'm making. Just sitting there and spinning yarns, and I'll be making more money than anybody else ever did for one night at A.A."

Skip glanced at him coldly. "You're right." He thought it over for a moment while he checked the stuff in his pockets, change and keys and cigarettes. "You never were a drunk. You're going to have to make it convincing."

"Oh, hell," Uncle Willy said cheerfully, "I had a cellmate in Quentin had been on every skid row from here to Brooklyn. The stories he told, I could keep gabbing for a week. You know, the damnedest thing, he said one time when he was in Seattle—at that time they didn't sell any liquor on Sunday, and this was Sunday—and he and some pals got some canned heat and strained it through a rag. Damned near blinded 'em."

A faint honk sounded from the street beyond Mr. Chilworth's house.

"That must be him," said Uncle Willy. He straightened his coat, picked his hat off the table, and ran out.

Skip listened to his dying footsteps with a sour look. He lit a cigarette, went into the bathroom for a last look at himself, ran the powder puff over his darkened jaw, snapped off the light. Outside in the alley the fragrance of the lime tree lay heavy on the air. There was no light at this point; the last traces of twilight, dying in the west, gave his hands on the lock a ghostly grayness. Skip opened the garage. Inside to the left was Mr. Chilworth's ancient Buick. Skip ran the jalopp out into the alley, closed the doors again, and drove away.

There was no way he could pay Uncle Willy back for bringing Big Tom into the job, or at least none at present. The loss of the money would have to suffice.

Karen was in the classroom, though the bell hadn't yet rung. She was sitting motionless before the typewriter. Skip slid into the empty chair in front of her, swinging a leg over so that he faced her, putting his hands on the chair back. "Hiya. Got the key?"

The little wing-like brows looked very dark against her pale skin, and her eyes, when she raised them, seemed buried in black lashes. "It wouldn't have done any good." Her voice was hoarse, and Skip caught the listless note and his attention sharpened. "She sent me downtown for the afternoon," Karen went on, "and when I got back there were all new locks on Stolz's room—the door, the windows too. I could see the new brass fixtures from the yard."

"How does she act to you?"

"I thought for a moment—" Karen bit her lip. "I thought she was going to talk to me about it."

Skip leaned closer, his stare narrowing. "How does she look at you? As if she thinks you're up to something? You'd catch that, wouldn't you?"

"She looks at me the way she always does."

"That's good." Skip thought about it, teetering on the legs of the chair. A few early arrivals were coming in; he lowered his tone to a whisper. "Look, I don't really care what kind of damned lock is on the door. Not tonight. This is the night we roll. If she's scared, scared enough to give us the key, good. If not—"

Karen seemed panic-stricken. "You'd let her see you?"

Skip nodded. "Why not? I'll fix it so she'll never recognize me."

Her hands fluttered on the keys of the machine. All color had left her face and her eyes burned with fright. "I won't let you in to hurt her or scare her."

Skip shrugged. "You getting ready to tip the old woman off?"

"I wouldn't do that."

"Look, you don't seem to understand the choice you've got here. You either line up with Eddie and me and help us in the house, or you tip off the old woman and she calls the bulls. There isn't going to be any way for you to chicken out, do nothing, keep your goddamn skirts clear." He reached, grabbed one of her hands, twisted the fingers painfully. "If you help us, you help all the way. See? A nice quick job, and we'll be cleared out and miles away by nine-thirty, if we leave class right at nine."

He got out of the chair and went quickly from the room. He had no doubts about Karen. Besides, he had an errand to do. He crossed the street from the school and entered a drugstore and asked to see some rubber gloves. If there had to be work done on that door they'd need these. He was particular, inspecting several pair. Finally he chose two pair, light in weight, in natural rubber, paid for them, stuffed the package into his jacket pocket. Too keyed up to return to class, he killed time then by strolling around and smoking cigarettes.

He didn't waste even a moment worrying about Mrs. Havermann and her new locks. You busted locks when you had to, and she was nothing. There was danger if she had called Stolz already, but this was a chance he had to take.

At a quarter of nine Eddie came out of class, having told the instructor a lie about a stomach-ache. He and Skip went for Karen. When she came out into the hall Eddie saw at once how bleak and depressed she looked, and he wanted to say something but held his tongue in front of Skip. At twelve minutes past nine they swung up the driveway of the Havermann house, motor cut and lights out. Skip guided the car into the dense shadow of some shrubbery. Skip and Eddie got out of the car, Karen dragging after them, and then Skip said to her, "Take off your stockings."

She didn't catch on at once, and Skip cursed her under his breath. Then when she had taken off her shoes and removed the nylon hose he and Eddie pulled a stocking apiece over their heads. Their features flattened weirdly, the skin whitening over the bones, eyes pinched up between folds of flesh. When Eddie looked at Skip he wanted to shudder.

Skip took the package from his pocket, removed the gloves, gave a pair to Eddie.

There were several lights on inside the house: the kitchen, upstairs, a room on the lower floor near the front of the house. "Now this is what you do," Skip said to Karen, his voice distorted and muffled by the flattening of his lips. "First, the dog. Shut him up where he won't get out, won't bark or bother us. Then come to the back door and fix it so we can get in. Then go and tell the old woman there's something she ought to look at in the kitchen. You smell gas leaking there, or something."

"She's going to be terribly scared," Karen protested. "Can't you do it some other way?"

"How? Now how could we do it another way?" Skip's manner was mild now, almost patient, but Eddie sensed the violence just under the surface, and Karen must have felt it too.

"Promise me," Karen got out, "that when she gives you the key you'll leave her alone. You won't hurt her."

"Now why would I do that?" Skip wondered.

"Promise," Karen insisted.

"Okay, okay. Now snap it up." Skip stretched inside the leather jacket as if he were almost bored. The light silk encasing his head gave him a strange brightness, almost a halo, in the dimness. It was crazy, Eddie thought, to think of Skip with a halo. Any time.

Karen walked away, the sound of her steps diminishing;

the dark swallowed her, and then a few moments later Eddie could hear the front door rattle. The interval following seemed unending to Eddie; he kept expecting some disastrous eruption of sound from the house, the old woman screaming, perhaps, as Karen betrayed their presence and their intention. He breathed thickly through the silk fabric pressing his face and felt as if he would choke.

Suddenly in the light reflected through the kitchen door they saw Karen in the porch. She fumbled with the lock, then moved quickly out of sight again. Skip turned toward Eddie and jerked his head in a summoning motion. They walked to the door. Eddie tried to lick his lips; his tongue snagged in the knitted silk and he was almost sick.

They went into the laundry room, not making any noise, and then Skip padded on into the kitchen and stood close to the wall on one side of the door to the hall and motioned Eddie to stand opposite. They hadn't been there more than a few seconds when Mrs. Havermann walked in. At the sight of the old woman, the realization that they were actually embarked on this thing, Eddie's heart gave a great lurch.

Mrs. Havermann went several feet past the door and then looked back over her shoulder. She glanced at Eddie, then switched her head all the way around to look at Skip. She turned a little, as if she meant to face them, and then her knees must have given out, for she reached a hand to prop herself against the table in the middle of the room.

"Who are you?" The words were plain enough in her high-pitched old woman's squeal, but they were mechanical and called for no reply. She knew who Eddie and Skip were: they were the double image of her nightmare, and her face shook and twitched at the shock of recognition. Then, "Go away!" she muttered in her throat. "Karen! Karen, send them away!"

Karen appeared in the hall. She was crying, making no attempt to wipe away the tears. She looked terribly young in her distress. She said, "I don't know what to do, Aunt Maude!" It had the ring of terrified truth.

Skip had put his hand in his jacket pocket, Eddie noticed, and had a finger poked forward to make it seem he held a gun. Eddie thought Mrs. Havermann was too stunned with fright to notice. She seemed ready to drop. As he watched, she actually tottered, then recovered. "Please don't . . . don't do anything violent," she stammered.

"That depends on you," Skip said in a perfectly indifferent manner. He was smiling a little, and the effect of the flesh moving and whitening under the knitted silk was uncanny. "We want the key to Stolz's room and then we want you to keep out of our way."

There was a moment of waiting while she made up her mind about it, or gained control of her shaking limbs, and then she slowly led the way out of the kitchen. They passed Karen, who shrank aside, then upstairs. At the top of the stairs Mrs. Havermann turned to face them. She seemed to have better control of herself. "You're wasting your time," she said to Skip. "There is nothing of value in Mr. Stolz's room."

"How about letting us see for ourselves?" Skip was easy and unworried. "Let's have the key, huh?"

Karen was about halfway up the stairs. She came on up

as Mrs. Havermann turned into her bedroom and opened a closet door. Skip tensed, perhaps thinking she had a gun hidden, but when she had fumbled for a moment in the pocket of a hanging coat she came out with the key. It had a new look; the ridges were sharp-cut. Skip grabbed it and nodded.

He glanced from Eddie to Karen. "Okay. Now tie her up."

Karen cried, "You promised!" and Skip said coolly, "Tie her up or I'll knock her out."

Mrs. Havermann licked her lips. "You tie me, Karen."

Skip was grinning twistedly inside the mask, and Eddie wondered if Karen knew how she had betrayed herself, crying out like that. Mrs. Havermann had a very thoughtful look as she sat down on the edge of the bed, where Skip motioned her. She looked as if she were thinking of things which had happened long ago, or over a long period of years. She looked as if there might be a bitter taste in her mouth.

"Turn over on the bed," Skip said to Mrs. Havermann. "Karen, tie her arms behind her. Tight. Wrists, then higher. And put juice in it."

"What shall I use?"

"For Chrissakes, tear up a towel or something."

Mrs. Havermann turned her head. "Karen, do you know these men?"

"I never saw them before," Karen answered, a confused childish lie. Everything she did showed that she knew Skip, was aware of his every move and glance. "What shall I use to tie you?"

"Don't destroy something good," Mrs. Havermann said,

much more calmly now. "Go to the linen closet and get one of the worn things."

Karen hurried out, came back in a moment with some pillowcases over her arm. She tore strips and tied Mrs. Havermann's arms and then, at Skip's orders, her ankles.

"Any cotton in the bathroom?" Skip demanded. "That fuzzy stuff."

"I guess so," Karen stammered, her eyes full of dread.

"Go see."

Karen backed around the edge of the bed, and Mrs. Havermann said in a low tone, "Please don't put a gag in my mouth. I promise I won't call out."

"Who's running this thing?" Skip inquired of the room. He went into the bathroom and came out with a blue box of absorbent cotton. He threw it on the bed. "Stuff her mouth with it. A rag over it to hold it." He looked at Karen, who hadn't moved.

"Please!" Mrs. Havermann gasped from where she lay. She had turned her eyes so that she could glimpse Skip. "I promise not to make a bit of trouble."

"You've got a choice," Skip said, unconcerned. "A gag. Or I'll clip you behind the ear and you won't see or hear anything for a while. Would you like that better?" He stepped forward, as if thinking she might really want him to knock her out, and she cringed on the counterpane, trying to inch her head away.

"No. No, I wouldn't want that."

"Okay. Karen, you'd better get busy." Skip regarded the shaking girl with a wry amusement. "Time's wasting."

Karen moved tremblingly nearer the older woman

and said uncertainly, "Will you open your mouth, Aunt Maude?"

"I'm not your aunt," Mrs. Havermann said, looking directly into Karen's eyes. "I wonder why I asked you to call me that. I wonder why I sheltered and fed you—now you've brought these two into my home."

Karen looked at Mrs. Havermann as if in an agony of regret.

"I don't know how you became acquainted with these two, the kind of creatures they seem to be. You've never been sly and secretive, slipping out at night, or acting in any way delinquent. You've seemed a straightforward girl. And now you've done this."

"Gag her, for Chrissakes," Skip said, his temper rising.

"The other one never says anything, does he?" Mrs. Havermann remarked harshly, looking at Eddie. Eddie knew that he was sweating through the silk mesh. It did not occur to him that his features were as distorted, as unreadable as Skip's.

Now Mrs. Havermann spoke directly to Eddie. "If you are sensible, young man, you'll leave now before a serious crime is committed."

An indignant growl escaped from Skip. He grabbed up a wad of cotton, and as Mrs. Havermann finished speaking he jabbed it between her teeth. Mrs. Havermann worked her jaws, trying to spit the cotton out, and then Karen rushed to pull it away and Skip straight-armed the girl back into the wall. He looked at Eddie.

"Take it easy, for Chrissakes," Eddie muttered.

Skip took a length of cotton cloth and wrapped it over

the lower part of Mrs. Havermann's face and tied it tight. Mumbling noises came through the gag. Mrs. Havermann's skin grew red, then darkened.

Skip said to Eddie, "Take Karen out in the hall."

Eddie went over to Karen. "She's passed out, she doesn't feel anything." He didn't want to look at Mrs. Havermann's flabby, suddenly sprawled body.

Karen was crouched against the wall, staring at Skip. "I'll have to stay with her. Don't touch me."

Skip held the key; he was tossing it, and the bright brass color sparkled in the light. "You're coming with us," he said to Karen. "I don't trust you much up here with the old woman. What the hell's the matter with you? I didn't do anything to her." He went to Karen and gripped her upper arm between his fingers, lifting her, and Eddie heard the gasp of pain she gave. "Now come along."

Karen went as if she were sleepwalking. Eddie was nervous, and Skip walked jauntily, snapping the key into the air and laughing under his breath. Skip unlocked the new lock on Stolz's door and they went in. Karen remained by the door. She seemed utterly indifferent now to the fascination of the money. Skip snapped on the light and hurried to the old-fashioned mahogany wardrobe against the inner wall. He stretched a hand to its door. The look of his curled fingers was hungry. He threw open the door and stood there blanked out with shock. Finally he looked at Eddie, then at the girl.

The wardrobe was empty.

Skip and Eddie searched hastily for the next few minutes, every cranny and hidey-hole in the room, expecting at any moment to run across the money. When it was obvious that the money wasn't in the room Skip would have turned on Karen. Eddie knew it, knew that his being here was the only thing which saved her from Skip's violence.

Trying to control his voice, Skip said to her, "We'll go back and see the old woman. Maybe you can get her to understand—we want the money Stolz kept here. We're going to get it."

Upstairs, they found Mrs. Havermann conscious again. Above the gag her eyes bugged at them.

Eddie felt hot and sick. He wished he had never seen the house or the old woman, never heard of the money.

It didn't occur to him to wish that he had never known Skip.

CHAPTER TWELVE

The city spread below the foothills made a great blaze in the sky and frosted the tips of the hills with reflected light; but here in the canyon it was dark, quiet except for the rustle of trees under the wind, and nothing moved except the small car creeping up the grade. The car rolled to a stop below Big Tom's house, the motor died, the lights went out, and a short stocky man in a black suit got out and looked all around. The only light in all that darkness was beside Tom's door.

Harry sniffed the breeze, noting the absence of exhaust fumes and city smoke. He looked back down the hill, toward the turnoff from the canyon highway. There was no traffic whatever. The canyon might have been a thousand miles from L.A. Big Tom had certainly picked him a spot.

Harry climbed to Big Tom's porch and rattled the screen door. The door within opened promptly. Big Tom was all dressed, ready to leave. A couple of cats were sitting attentively in the middle of the room, looking at their master as if wondering what possible business he had out at this hour.

"Just a minute. I want to check the back door." Big Tom started away, and the phone began ringing. Big Tom ignored it, went into the kitchen for a minute, then came back. Harry had his head inside, holding the screen ajar with his shoulder.

"Aren't you going t' answer the damned phone?"

"I know who it is. Benny." Big Tom walked by the table where the phone sat, didn't give it a glance. "To hell with him."

"Maybe he knows something," Harry said. "Maybe you ought t' hear what he says, anyhow."

"I know what he says. He's been saying it all day."

"Well, then, maybe I ought t' hear what he says," Harry declared. A touch of truculence had come into his manner. He stepped into the room.

Big Tom gave him a cool stare. "Are you going with me, or aren't you?"

"I might be going, after I hear from Benny. He saved me one hell of a blowup in Frisco. I just want t' hear what he says."

"Oh, hell, go ahead and listen." Big Tom sat down on a chair and folded his hands between his knees and looked unlovingly at the cats sitting together in the middle of the rug.

Harry went to the phone and lifted it out of its cradle and put it to his ear. "Yeah. No, this is Harry. We're ready t' roll." He listened and pretty soon his tongue came out and licked at his lips. "You think it's on the level?"

The silence made a cup, a kind of vacuum, around the house, and Big Tom sat moveless as if he might be listening for some scratch of sound, the tiniest indication of a break in that envelopment. He didn't look at Harry. Harry's nervous fright rolled from him in waves, like a smell.

Harry put the phone into its cradle, went to a chair facing Big Tom, sat down. "My God," he said. He took out a white linen handkerchief and mopped at his neck under the collar. "What a hell of a break." Big Tom made no reply, showed no curiosity, just waited; and Harry went on: "All day Benny's been following this character, buying him drinks and trying t' chum him up . . . when he wasn't ducking out t' phone you . . . and he finally got the character drunk enough and he talked. He talked about Stolz."

Big Tom grabbed one of his cats and inspected behind its ears for fleas. He didn't look in Harry's direction.

"This boy Benny's been with is a real hard-nose. Tough. Benny thinks he's a gun from El Paso, somebody he met once. Worked for Stolz for a year or so. Not working for him now. Uses a different moniker. Won't be needing any moniker at all if he blabs much what he's been blabbing t' Benny."

"Well, I'm glad you're working around to the big news," Big Tom said.

"The news is bad, real bad," Harry answered, his eyes shining like wet soap. "The word is that Stolz bought a chunk of the Hartfield ransom. Got it for about ten cents on the dollar. No bargain at that. You remember about the Hartfields?"

Big Tom put the cat down carefully on all four feet. "Yeah, I remember."

"The job was a ripperoo all the way around," Harry

went on breathlessly. "The punks who snatched Hartfield and his wife didn't have sense enough t' specify the kind of money. So they got hundreds, all consecutive, every goddamn number taped— Oh, my god! And we nearly walked int' that!"

Big Tom lifted his eyes slowly. "You're not going?"

"Good God! Good God!" Harry cried loudly. "You're not going either!"

"Yes, I am."

Harry lowered his face and peered at Big Tom as through a haze. "Now, now wait up—"

"I'm going," Big Tom affirmed. "I didn't know it myself until just now. I kept thinking all day, if Benny dug up something smelly I'd have to drop it, but then I quit answering the phone so I wouldn't hear what he said. All the time I knew I was going and didn't realize I'd made up my mind. Till now."

"What in the blazing hell," Harry wondered, his mouth puckering, "can you do with dough as hot as that?"

"Stolz must have had a plan for it," Big Tom said. "Maybe I can figure out what it was, use it myself." He stood up, checked his keys, adjusted the gun inside his belt against his belly. He said as if to himself, excluding Harry, "I'll have to go it alone."

"You sure will," Harry agreed.

Big Tom walked over to the door. "Will you phone Snope for me?"

"He'll blow his stack. They don't want hot moola!"

"It's his cut anyway," Big Tom said. "Hot or cold." He had a look of ironic amusement as he went out, not even bothering to shut the door. Harry sat for a minute or more as if undecided. He plucked at his lip. He heard Tom's Ford, first inside the garage down by the road, warming up, then out in the open. Finally Harry stood up, went to the front door to listen. The sounds of Tom's car died in the distance, and Harry shook his head in relief.

He said to the listening cats, "He's crazy as a bedbug. He ought t' be in the loony bin."

Harry went out, snapping the lock but leaving all the lights on. The cats wandered around the room for a brief while, annoyed at being alone, then settled in the shabby chairs to sleep.

And then after all, along with the terrific fright there was desperate defiance. Mrs. Havermann had had time to gather her forces somewhat. When Skip had taken out enough of the cotton wadding so that she could speak she croaked, "Mr. Stolz is on his way here. I'm doing you a favor by telling you. When he comes he won't stand for any nonsense, and he certainly won't let you take his money!"

For the first time Skip's assurance slipped. He grabbed Mrs. Havermann by the shoulders and dragged her up and shook her. "When? When's he coming?" Karen, trying to interfere, got in his way then, and he jabbed viciously with an elbow, still hanging onto Mrs. Havermann. Karen gave a cry and put a hand to her cheek. "When? When is Stolz coming?"

"Any minute now." She was tied, helpless, and the nerves twitched in her face, but she kept her eyes angrily on Skip. "You'd better leave at once."

Perhaps she thought she really had frightened him. Skip grew quiet, bent over the bed, his foxy eyes suddenly still and watchful. So she pressed it a little further. "I believe I hear Mr. Stolz at the front door downstairs now."

The three of them waited, frozen, listening for some sound from below. Skip went softly out into the hall, listened, came back. "She's giving us a line of crap. I'm going to work her over."

Karen flung herself between him and Mrs. Havermann. "Don't hurt her! You promised. I wouldn't have let you in if you hadn't promised!"

Mrs. Havermann writhed up on one elbow and the head of the bedstead. "Karen, look at me." When Karen had turned, Mrs. Havermann went on: "I don't want you pleading for me. I don't want a word from you in my behalf. You no longer mean anything to me. The love and loyalty I might have expected from you are as ashes. I want nothing from you. You owe me nothing." Tears filled Karen's eyes, ready to spill; and then Mrs. Havermann forced her head forward a little, and from between the cotton-flecked lips she spat into Karen's face.

Skip laughed. Eddie moved to the rim of the room, anxious, hating the delay, hating his own feelings of fear and inadequacy.

"Why do we take time to argue?" Eddie said. "She's hidden the money to save it for Stolz. So we find it. We don't have to hurt anybody."

"In this place we find it?" Skip hollered.

"Karen can help. She'll know the places it could be hidden."

Karen had gone away from Mrs. Havermann and the bed. She had wiped the spit off her face with her sleeve. At the moment Mrs. Havermann had leaned forward and spat, a look of unbelieving shock had flooded Karen. But now she seemed to have regained a dull composure.

"How about it?" Skip demanded of Karen.

She looked around at them, at Eddie and Skip. She didn't look at Mrs. Havermann. "Yes, I guess so."

They split up. Karen said she'd take the attic and the upper bedrooms, let Eddie and Skip search the easier area downstairs. There was a basement too, she told them; nothing in it but the oil furnace, though they'd have to check.

In the kitchen, in a lower cupboard behind a stack of canned dog food, Skip found two packets of hundred-dollar bills. For an instant he was about to let out a shout, thinking he'd located the hoard; but then in sizing it up he noted that the two packets were out of the way in a dark spot, as if Mrs. Havermann might have started to put the money in there and then changed her mind, retrieving what she had stored. These two packets had escaped her searching fingers.

Skip, wary for steps outside the kitchen door, flipped through the money. It looked new. He studied it closely; it wasn't counterfeit; the bills were perfect. He noted a number on a bill, then two, then three. This new money was numbered consecutively, as if it might have just come from the mint. Skip shook his head and grinned. Stolz had converted something—surplus profits, a payoff, a sale of shares —into this easily stored and beautifully legitimate currency. The newness of the bills, the consecutive numbering were to Skip an indication that there was nothing wrong here. Stolz had his cash where he could get it and spend it easily if he wanted to. He'd just forgotten to keep an eye on it!

Skip rose, having made sure there were no other packets scattered in the depths of the cupboard. He put the two packets inside his shirt against his skin, buttoned his shirt over them. He kept on smiling to himself, the smile distorted by the silken mask. The old woman hadn't been so smart after all. She was just a stupid, panicky old bag, putting new locks on doors and then getting scared the locks weren't enough and trying a trick or two. She was the kind of old bag would keep dimes and quarters in a sugar bowl. He wished he could go up and be allowed to punch her face in.

He happened to be looking toward the door when Eddie appeared there. "I've been thinking about what Mrs. Havermann said about Stolz," Eddie told Skip. "If he's really on his way here, apt to arrive any time, it might be better to have Mrs. Havermann out of sight."

Skip regarded him thoughtfully.

"If he comes in," Eddie continued, "you and I could hear him in time to slip out the other door. Then if he caught Karen upstairs she could pretend nothing was wrong, the old lady was out seeing some friends or something. If she wasn't out where he could see her, tied up like that, he'd have no way of knowing right off that anything was going on."

"Sure, you're right." They went down the hall, passing the open door of the parlor where Eddie had been searching. Karen met them at the top of the stairs. Skip stopped and said, "We're going to put Mrs. Havermann out of sight. So if Stolz comes he won't see her right away. And you can tell him she's out visiting, until you have a chance to slip out."

Karen started to say something. Probably she intended to remind Skip again of his promise that there would be no violence. But the words died before she spoke them. She looked tired and drawn. Her cheek was swelling where Skip had struck her with his elbow. There was a deeper wound somewhere inside; her eyes were sick with the pain of it.

Skip said to Karen, "Stay out here and keep an eye on that front door while we're in there."

Skip actually wasn't much scared that Stolz would arrive; he thought that Mrs. Havermann had made up a yarn to frighten them. But he had begun to worry a little about Big Tom and his friends. They had to be out of here before Big Tom arrived.

On the bed Mrs. Havermann lay with her eyes shut. Her mouth was pinched and she seemed pale, almost bluish. "We'll put the gag back," Skip said, gathering up the scattered cotton.

Mrs. Havermann opened her eyes. "You are a wicked person," she said. "God knows what you are doing here; He sees your every act. And He will punish you for it."

For some reason it triggered Skip's rage. He bent over her and slapped her hard and repeatedly. He had his fists doubled then, ready to pump blows into her face, when Eddie dragged him away. Eddie was yelling, "*Sancta Maria!*"

and in a flood of Spanish he commanded Skip to leave her alone, not even realizing which tongue he used. He and Skip stood with their eyes not more than a couple of feet apart, and he heard Skip calling him a half-Mex bastard, and then he knew what he had said.

"Chrissakes, don't beat up an old woman!" he told Skip.

"What was all that yap in Mex?"

"Just that. Don't hurt her."

Skip showed his teeth through the silk mask. "She knows where that money is."

"Well—just ask her, then."

"Ah, she'd never tell us." By main force Skip got the wadding of cotton back into Mrs. Havermann's unwilling mouth. He pushed it in hard, then wrapped her face in the piece of cloth.

"Not too tight," Eddie warned.

"She'll keep her yap shut now," Skip said savagely, giving the wrapping another knot.

Eddie was uneasy, but he didn't want another fight with Skip. He went to the closet door, opened it, and looked in. It was a big closet, neatly arranged, well filled with clothing. Skip inched Mrs. Havermann off the bed, carrying her by the shoulders, and he and Eddie got her into the closet under the hanging garments. She struggled and bumped around, made frantic muffled noises under the gag. Skip stood and watched interestedly from the closet doorway.

Eddie said nervously, "Please, Mrs. Havermann, just lie still. We won't bother you again. Mr. Stolz will come and find you, and you'll be all right."

Mrs. Havermann thrashed and convulsed. Her thick legs whipped back and forth with surprising force, scattering some shoes set in a row along the closet wall.

"She acts like she's having a doggone fit," Skip said musingly.

A shrill noise now came from under the gag, as if Mrs. Havermann had swallowed a toy whistle. The whipping motion of her lower limbs was slowing down. She tried to push herself erect by means of her bound hands, but soon fell back.

Eddie had gone out of the room. "You just take a nice little nap," Skip said to Mrs. Havermann, and kicked her foot back into the closet and shut the door.

They went back to the search. Skip looked through Mrs. Havermann's room before leaving it, inspecting a sewing box, a big basket of mending, a small black trunk. Everything the old woman owned, he thought, stank of moth balls. When he lifted the trunk lid the odor was almost stifling. He noted that in the top tray there lay a large framed photograph, the picture of a stout man with an autocratic and arrogant expression.

Havermann, he thought.

He rifled the trunk, threw stuff back into it, shut the lid. Hell, there was no money in this room. Nor in this part of the house, either. He thought about the cupboard where he'd found the two packets hidden behind the dog food. There ought to be a clue there. Something had made her change her mind. She'd thought of a better spot. Skip tried to figure out what there was about the cupboard or the stored dog food to remind her of some better place, tried to think as Mrs. Havermann would have thought, and failed. Neither the cupboard nor the dog food reminded him of a thing.

There was an especially loud thump from the closet, as if Mrs. Havermann had made one last try for the door with a heel. Then there was silence.

Skip left the room, went downstairs, and then, taking care to move silently, he went out into the rear yard. He needed to reassure himself that Big Tom wasn't out there. He scouted around the car, looked down the driveway to the street. It would be a hell of a note if Big Tom showed up and caught them here in the middle of the search. Skip pulled off the stocking from his face, smoked a cigarette, sheltering the lighted tip inside his palm, watching the street and trying to think his way past the stalemate. The old woman had outfoxed them, beaten them. Skip hissed the killdeer cry between his teeth and thought of what he would like to do to her.

All at once he saw Eddie in the porch used as a laundry room. Eddie moved over to the door and peered out and said, "Skip, we've got to get out of here!"

Skip walked toward him, pulling on the mask. "You can say that again," he growled.

"I've been thinking. Mrs. Havermann's going to have to tell us. Not by hurting her. But we could threaten to do something. Like burn the house down."

"Okay. What happens if she doesn't bite?"

"Maybe she'll bite," Eddie said hopefully.

They went back through the hall to the stairs. Karen was there, standing as if all life, all emotion, had drained out of her. Her eyes seemed set deep in her head, burned dark with strain. She said in a little above a whisper, "Let her go, Skip."

"Sure," Skip agreed. "We're going to let her go. Right now." He ran up the stairs with Eddie following, and crossed Mrs. Havermann's room and threw open the closet door. Mrs. Havermann's contorted form fell out into the room, dragging some fallen clothes with her. Somehow, after he'd shut the door on her, she'd writhed around to lie against it. Skip bent over her, got a good look at her, and he knew.

Mrs. Havermann was dead.

CHAPTER THIRTEEN

Skip and Eddie looked at the dead, contorted face and then slowly at each other; and the silence was like the ear-bursting backslap of an explosion or like the vast sucking up after a great wind had passed or like the final stillness after the toppling of a tidal wave.

Eddie said unbelievingly, "I stood right here and let you do it!"

"What do you mean, let *me* do it?" Skip's mouth thinned to an ugly line and his hands balled to fists. "Hell, you were in it; you helped me get her into the closet where she suffocated."

"You murdered her," Eddie said slowly.

Skip's fists knotted tightly, and he knocked Eddie down with one blow. Eddie had been dazed, not looking, too shocked to react, to protect himself. He hit the wall and slid down, and then in an automatic response to terror he started to scramble for the door. Skip had run out swiftly. He collided with Karen at the top of the stairs, and they half fell part of the way down before they could stop and disentangle themselves. Karen cried, "What's wrong up there? What's happened?" Her face was wild with fear.

"Go to hell." Skip stiff-armed her, and she toppled away and staggered on down to the lower hall.

Eddie came out of the room, got to his feet, stood there hanging horrified on the railing. He looked down at Karen. "She's dead. The gag was too tight, and it choked her to death."

Karen gave a choked scream and tried to run back up the stairs, and again Skip stiff-armed her and she backed away, crying breathlessly, holding her stomach.

"We're leaving, you sap. Aren't you coming?" Skip said to her.

He ran past her, on down the hall. Eddie came downstairs quickly. Karen looked at him with stunned, uncomprehending eyes and said, "It isn't true, is it? She's all right."

"She's dead." He saw the shock of these words go through her like a blow, draining her skin of color, her eyes of life. There wasn't time for gentleness, but Eddie had to be gentle with her. He put an arm around her. "Don't go back and look at her. Not if you liked her, and I guess you did."

She said: "Liked her? I loved her. I just never could . . . She never let me show her." She covered her face then and would have wept against him, but Eddie pushed her gently away.

"We've got to leave. Quick. Come on."

He took her hand, and she let him lead her out through the rear door. At the car Skip had stripped off mask and gloves and was inside fitting the key into the switch. Eddie and Karen ran around to the other side and got in, Karen in the middle.

Skip started the motor, and then it coughed gently and

died. He tried again, nursing it, giving it gas, and Eddie could hear the tired sparkless rattle as it turned over without catching, and the noise of loose fittings and the gradual wearing down of the battery. And over all this, Karen's exhausted crying.

Eddie had stripped off the stocking from his face, the gloves. He was sweating now; his heart was pounding. The old motor ground and ground, and each time it turned over the sound was weaker and more dragging.

Skip looked at them jeeringly. "Anybody got any suggestions?"

"For Chrissakes get it started," Eddie said.

The motor caught for a second time, hesitated for an instant that seemed an eternity, and then settled into its rackety rhythm. Eddie let out a long aching breath, unaware that he'd even been holding it.

The car slipped down the drive in the dark, and once in the street Skip switched on the lights and let it pick up speed.

Eddie said hotly, "I wish I'd never heard of that goddamn money."

"We just had bad luck, that's all," Skip answered evenly. He was beginning to calm down somewhat, to reconsider what had really happened. He didn't believe their situation to be completely hopeless. It was too bad of course that they couldn't leave Karen here to palm off some yarn to the homicide dicks about strange, unknown men breaking in and killing Mrs. Havermann and mistreating herself. In his present mood he was more than ready to mark Karen up to leave the right impression with the cops. But he had no illusions about Karen standing up under questioning. She was too young and soft, too easily hurt. Skip jerked his head over his shoulder in the direction of the house. "Well, good-by Stolz's dough, wherever you are." He laughed a little under his breath.

Karen tried to draw away from him. "How can you make a joke . . . how can you act as if nothing had happened?"

"You and Eddie go ahead and tear your hair and squall," Skip said. "Me, I've got to drive the jalopp. It's never learned to drive itself. And I can't see to drive if I'm crying."

He had turned into the busy boulevard. A big transit bus rolled by, a scattering of people in it, tired faces turned to the windows. In a rear seat a small wrinkled hatless man looked especially discouraged and weary. His eyes were almost covered with drooping, parchment-like lids. As the car gathered speed, Skip found himself staring up at the bus window, keeping pace; and the wheel wobbled between his hands.

"Hey!" Eddie said. "Watch it, we don't want a ticket now."

The bus sped on, and they kept abreast of the rear window. Skip could see the tired, wrinkled face just above; the washed-out old eyes seemed dead beneath the parchment lids. "Look at that," Skip said between his teeth. "Look at this old geezer by the window. You know what?"

"What?" said Eddie uneasily. He couldn't see the old man from where he sat, but he heard the anger in Skip's tone.

"We had a chance," Skip said. "The old woman ruined it for us, the only decent chance we'll ever have."

"It's over," Eddie said, his tone hardening. "We were lucky to get out."

"All we needed was the dough," Skip went on. "She didn't have to act like a son of a bitch over it. She could have co-operated a little."

He glanced up again at the bus window. The old man sat with his forehead sagging toward the window, his tired eyes fixed on nothing. He had glanced once at Skip, almost sharply, but now seemed withdrawn again into his private limbo. He had only the night, the passing cars, the gloomy and uninteresting way home. He was the kind of old man who existed in an endless rut. Lives in some rattrap rooming house, Skip thought. His feet hurt. He must have a job where he stood up all day. Maybe he was a dishwasher. Skip pictured the old man over a steamy sink, scraping garbage, stewing his hands for hour after hour in hot soapy water. Once in a while ducking out to a littered alley for a cigarette. What a life, what a dirty rotten break. Such rage rose in Skip that he had difficulty in keeping it under control.

The through boulevard swung to the east in a slight curve. In the distance, across vacant rising ground, the Havermann house among its trees glittered with light. Eddie said, "Oh, for God's sake, look at it. Like a Christmas tree! Why didn't we turn off the lights?"

"Yeah, why didn't you?" Skip said.

"What do the lights matter?" Karen cried as if bewildered.

They were passing the hamburger diner when Skip braked the car sharply and turned in at the parking lot.

"You're not . . . stopping?" Karen gasped.

"I'm hungry as hell," Skip said. "I didn't get any dinner. My unc was too worked up to cook anything for me."

"What was he worked up about?" Eddie said quickly, suspiciously.

It had been a slip, but Skip didn't worry about it. He parked the car and cut the motor, took the keys from the lock. "Ah, he was going to an A.A. meeting for the first time."

"I didn't know he drank," Eddie said, still curious.

"Well . . ." Skip spoke with mock reluctance. "God knows Unc should have learned better by now, but I think he's planning some sort of con on those A.A. people. He thinks he'll get their sympathy, sing them a hard-luck story, maybe cop a little dough."

"They'll know right away he's a phony," Eddie said positively.

"I don't see how you can worry about Skip's uncle and whether he drinks or not and what he's doing with the A.A. people," Karen said with frantic urgency. "If we don't want to be caught . . . just please, please don't stop here!"

Skip glanced at her. "Well, it's good to see that you've started to collect your marbles. You're worrying about getting away instead of about the old woman. But you're right in a way—someone might know you, this close to home. So you stay in the car, and Eddie can stay with you while I go in and have a bite." He got out, brushed back his hair where the stocking mask had disarranged it, and walked away across the graveled lot.

He sat over a hamburger and coffee, frowning in thought. He couldn't get the image of the old man in the bus out of his mind. There seemed some sort of carry-over, some connection with himself. A threat.

The old man who swamped dishes in the diner came out and began to clean the counter. Skip watched him, thinking that this old character with the gray face and the white tee shirt resembled in some way the old man on the bus and seeing that the pattern could have been laid out to enfold himself.

In the car Karen was weeping on Eddie's shoulder, and Eddie held her, at first loosely and then more closely, feeling the shudders that racked her young bones beneath her flesh.

Big Tom parked two blocks from the house, down the boulevard where there were a liquor store and a drugstore, both open, and a closed barbershop and shoeshine stand. He parked his car out of the direct light, went into the drugstore, and looked around, walked out quickly, went briskly away down the dark sidewalk to the cross street. He strolled uphill, eyes and ears alert. When he finally got within sight of the Havermann house and saw all the lights in it, he was filled with a ravaging disappointment. It had all the signs of a four-bell alarm.

Still he continued, drawn by bitter frustration, and walked on past. He had expected to see cars in the driveway, indications that the police were there, but it all seemed quiet enough. Not a soul moved in the grounds.

A full-fledged conviction had come into his mind that Skip and his friend had moved in early, forestalling him, had botched it and been discovered by the old woman. Now he wasn't so sure.

On an impulse he ducked into the heavy shrubbery

bordering the drive, crouched there, waited. He could hear a dog barking in the distance, perhaps inside the house. There was no other sound at all. He pushed further into the shrubs and came out into a sort of lane, overhung by dusty evergreens and ditched for irrigation purposes, which led up directly to the house. Big Tom stole forward, careful to make no noise, and in a couple of minutes he had sized up the house, both front and rear, and was more puzzled than ever.

He retreated into the shadowy darkness to figure things out. It seemed now that no public alarm had been given; the place was much too silent for that. The old woman might be inside, scared, with all the lights on, having been alarmed by some preliminary boobery by Skip. Or—his mind seized on a new idea—Skip and his friend might be in there searching, the old woman having outwitted them somehow.

Stolz could be there, of course, a grimmer possibility to Big Tom than the presence of the police. Big Tom chewed a lip, squinted at the lights, considered thoughtfully.

Common sense and every instinct for danger he possessed warned him to get out of here, forget the job, forget he'd ever heard of the old house and the money in it. But Big Tom hesitated. He was curious. His hands itched for the money, the great beautiful green heap—hot or not.

All at once he caught a movement at an upper window, stiffened, his eyes narrowed with fright. Something yellow bobbed against the pane, an indistinct furry mass; and then the dog had his paws on the window sill and seemed to be peering out at the dark and barking as if to summon help.

"Now that's a funny thing," Big Tom said under his breath. He waited, and the dog bounced there, pawing at the pane, and the echo of his barking drifted out upon the night. "He's shut in. He's raising hell about it."

Big Tom went on thinking. If the old woman was in there scared, with the lights on to drive away potential prowlers, she wouldn't have the dog shut up that way. The dog would be downstairs, or outside, watching the place.

If Skip and Eddie were in there, though, messing around, shutting the dog up out of the way would be the first thing they'd do.

A faint smile touched Big Tom's lips. He pushed the dark cap back off his head a little; a few locks of the stiff gray hair escaped. He scratched around at his hairline. "By God, that must be it. They're in there doing something. Or they've just left." The thought that they might have just escaped with the money sent Big Tom hurrying from the bushes to the back door. He stopped there, took an old pair of gloves from his pants pocket, and slipped them on his hands. He patted the gun against his belly. Then he tried the screen door. It opened under his touch.

Like a man made of smoke, he drifted silently through the outer porch, glancing at the washing machine and the tubs in passing, and entered the kitchen and paused to listen. The dog's barking echoed sharply from upstairs. He couldn't hear another sound. No voices, footsteps, no clatter of struggle or search. He wondered briefly if the house, except for the disturbed dog, could be entirely empty.

With the greatest caution he crept into the hall. He saw the open door of the pantry, the light burning within, the sewing room across the hall, beyond these more doors, and then, at a point where the hall turned in a right angle, the edge of a hall runner and a bright glow from above. He recalled the location of Stolz's room as described by Skip, and noted that ahead and to the right a closed door had a bright, brass-colored, apparently new lock set into the wood.

Walking softly, walking on the edges of his shoes, he went to the door and tried the knob; the door opened at once. Inside the light burned in the overhead fixture. His gaze swept the room and took in the wardrobe, the open door of its clothes compartment gaping on nothing, the spilled drawers and other signs of search. Alarm caught him, froze him in the doorway. Everything seemed to hammer to a stop inside him: his heart, his breath, thought itself. He stood arrested by fright, gawking, until he remembered the hall and his unprotected back and moved on into the room.

He went over to the wardrobe and looked at it for a moment and then touched it with his gloved hand, shutting the little door. He looked around then, and certain facts occurred to him. If the money had been where Skip had expected it to be, there wouldn't have been a search.

The search had been successful, though, or they'd still be here.

It occurred to Big Tom to wonder where Mrs. Havermann was.

He stood in the middle of the room, undecided, listening for any scratch of sound. The sense of warning drilled through him again, but he resisted it. The curiosity was like a nagging itch inside his brain. He wanted to see what was in the rest of the house, make sure what had happened here, allay the hope that the money might remain.

He waited for another minute, listening to the creaking stillness punctuated now and then by the dog's yapping, and then went back into the hall.

Skip walked out to the car and approached it opposite the driver's seat. He heard Eddie say something, and Karen lifted her head and smoothed her hair; and a slight smile touched Skip's mouth, increasing the foxy look, narrowing his thin lips. He stood close to Eddie's door, and Eddie rolled down the glass.

"I'm going back," Skip said.

The two in the car looked out as if not understanding what he'd said. Karen's wet eyes gleamed in the dimness. All at once Eddie caught on and said, "Chrissakes, for why? You must be nuts."

"Ah, I just . . ." Skip's manner was completely relaxed. "I just want one more chance. The dough's there. Got to be."

"But she's dead in there," Karen said, leaning past Eddie, her voice shaking. "You can't go back!"

"Yell a little louder," Skip encouraged. "I don't think they quite heard that in the diner."

"Please! Please—let's not go back," she begged.

"Like I say," he went on, "the money's in there, maybe lying some perfectly ordinary place we just forgot to look at, some place I'd notice right away if I went back."

"You're crazy," Eddie said. "How do you know the cops aren't there right now?"

"Why should they be?" Skip demanded.

"Didn't you hear what she said about Stolz coming?" Eddie's nervous tension made his words jump.

"Ah, she just made it up to get rid of us." There was a moment of silence and then Skip said, "You remember what Karen told us, she was kind of sweet on Stolz? Hell, she must have been. She died trying to save his dough for him."

Karen cried brokenly then, and Eddie was distracted, trying to comfort her. He looked around, found that Skip had opened the door beside him. "We're going to change places. You'll do the driving now. You're going to drive by and drop me off at those trees. I'll work my way back to the house."

Eddie got out, went around the car. It was absolute insanity to stay in the neighborhood, much less go anywhere near that house. He wondered in an instant of self-revelation why he let Skip dictate this crazy course to him.

Skip got in on the other side of the car, shut the door. "Give me thirty minutes. I'll come out the same way, through the trees. If I'm not there give me another half hour before you come back again. But go by the house, size it up, before you stop anywhere either time."

"What'll we do?"

Skip looked slyly from Eddie to Karen. "Just drive around. And keep out of trouble."

CHAPTER FOURTEEN

Uncle Willy was surprised, a little disappointed, to see what a large gathering it was. The place was a grammar school auditorium. He and his sponsor slipped into their seats just as the proceedings opened. A big husky-looking guy on the stage at the front of the room rapped a gavel on a table and said, "Will the meeting please come to order?"

Willy looked all around. He had to make enough of an impression here so that he would be remembered, his time accounted for. A smaller group would have been better, easier to handle.

The chairman waited until the rustling and whispering subsided. Then, looking directly and rather fixedly at the people nearest the platform, he said, "Good evening, folks. My name is Jerry. I'm an alcoholic."

The audience answered in unison, "Hello, Jerry."

"He's an alcoholic?" Willy whispered to Mitchell. Willy thought he'd never seen a healthier specimen in his life than the man in front of the room. Mitchell nodded, smiling encouragement.

"He got his five-year pin a couple of weeks ago," Mitchell replied.

Jerry, the chairman, now said, "You all know Betty. Betty, will you please open our meeting by reading the twelve steps?"

Betty stood up in the front row, turned around holding the A.A. manual. She was a woman of around thirty, smartly dressed, rather good-looking. She read the twelve steps of the A.A. program in a firm clear voice.

"That's another one?" Willy wondered, squinting at her.

"Look," Mitchell said, "this is a closed meeting. Everybody here has been through the mill. Some of these people would be dead if it weren't for A.A. All these people, sober and presentable, interested in helping each other, were once just as confused and lost as you are."

On the way here Willy had given Mitchell a line composed equally of imagination and the recollections of his old cellmate. Now he wondered if he might have overdone it a little. No matter. Mitchell's expression was friendly, and he was safely in the midst of a group with all their wits about them. Willy nodded to Mitchell and gave his attention to the program.

The speaker of the evening had come all the way from Riverside to be with them. He came forward smiling after Jerry's introduction, a stocky man nearly bald, and looked out over the audience and said, "Yes, folks, this is me—Bob. I'm an alcoholic. Hello, everybody."

The murmur responded from the listeners, "Hello, Bob."

As a preamble, Bob began: "Whenever I address a meeting like this I always wonder how many first-timers there are to hear what I have to say. I'd like to see hands of any first-timers here tonight."

Mitchell glanced at Willy, smiling. Willy raised his hand. A woman down the row, who had a hatbrim pulled over her eyes as if afraid she might be recognized, also put up her hand.

Bob counted the scattering of hands. "Six. Well, that's fine. I'm especially interested in you beginners. If I could, to encourage you, I'd turn the clock back and show you, for a couple of minutes, how I looked, acted, and felt just three years ago." Bob shook his head over the memory. Then his voice hoarsened, took on an edge of authority. "I was a bum," he stated bluntly. "I was down in the gutter. I *mean* gutter—I laid in it or near it night after night right here in L.A. skid row. I was a thief, too. Anything I could find that wasn't nailed down I sold to a junk dealer for money to buy wine. I panhandled. I rolled other drunks. I'd have stolen the dimes off my dead grandmother's eyes if I could have gotten to them. Lucky for her, my grandmother is perfectly healthy and lives in Iowa. She never knew what a close call she had."

The audience responded with a ripple of mirth. The stocky balding man had won his listeners. What he lacked in skill as a speaker he more than made up in sincerity and force. In spite of a determined inward cynicism and a wish to disassociate himself and daydream over the money, Willy found himself engrossed and impressed. My God, what the man had done with himself was almost unbelievable!

Bob went on to tell other details of his life as an alcoholic. His attitude was without bitterness, had instead a rather clinical air of reflection. Somehow, Willy sensed, Bob had made peace with whatever demons had driven him.

Bob related incidents which in other company would have been the cause of raised eyebrows, the bum's rush, or even calling the cops. He confessed to crimes committed under the influence of drink, horrible involvements with other skid-row denizens, blackouts, jail sentences, narrow escapes from death. His audience listened tolerantly, respectfully, laughing once in a while, and occasionally someone would nod as if an anecdote had hit home.

Bob told of the loss of home, family, and friends. His wife had deserted him early in his downward progress. His mother and father had forbidden him ever to set foot in their home. His brothers and sisters refused to recognize him on the street.

"In skid row and in jail I seemed to have come home at last," Bob said. "The environment made a kind of shelter, taking the place of all I had lost through alcoholism. I knew I couldn't adjust to normal people, normal surroundings. I kept myself stupefied on drink and stayed where I felt at home—in the gutter."

Willy was almost overwhelmed with a sense of compassionate brotherhood. True, he'd never been a drunk. Thievery had been his compulsion, separating him from decent companions and decent surroundings as effectively as liquor had done for Bob. In Willy's mind he translated what Bob had said into circumstances which applied to himself and was astounded at the parallel.

Bob's voice dropped to a confidential, hopeful note. "Well, one night when it seemed all that was left to me was a wretched death and a drunkard's grave," he went on, "by accident I found myself in the back room of a mission where an A.A. meeting was going on. I don't remember how I got into the place. I think I might have gone in there with the idea of stealing a snooze under a bench—out of sight of the mission people, who might have wanted me to bathe and eat and get my clothes laundered. I needed a bath. Yes, I remember that much. I noticed that a bum, almost as bad-looking a bum as I was, moved away when I sat too close to him."

Bob smiled cheerfully over the memory, and the audience smiled with him. Willy felt something run down his cheek from the corner of his eye. He put up an inquiring finger, found a damp streak. Oh, God, he was crying! Making an ass of himself! At the same moment he felt Mitchell's hand patting his arm. Willy wanted to run.

Bob continued: "And so, stinking and sick, hardly able to sit erect on the bench, I waited out the meeting. Somehow —this was a miracle—some of the meaning of the A.A. program got through to me. I got to talking to the bum who had moved away on the bench. He said he'd been a member for three weeks now and had tapered down to one quart of wine a day."

The audience laughed.

Bob waited until the amusement subsided. "When the meeting was over I went up to the front of the room and collared the speaker and said something to him—I don't remember what. This man, someone I'd never seen before and have never seen again—took time to sit down and discuss my problems with me. He urged me to stay at the mission, get some rest, clean up. He even—now get this

—he even offered to take me home with him to help me straighten up."

There was a silence now, a few sighs. Willy thought, My God, that guy was a sucker, offering to take a drunk home, maybe get his place torn up by a maniac with the D.T.s. At the same time, the generosity of the offer touched him immensely, and he sensed that it had made a great change in Bob.

Bob continued soberly, "In the days that followed, while I wandered in a drunken haze, the thought of this man's trust and confidence kept coming back. Finally I returned to the A.A. meeting on another night at the mission. I won't try to fool you and say that I changed overnight or never had any trouble with liquor afterwards, or any such lies. It was tough. There were days when I didn't think I could make it."

Willy was shaking his head now, trembling. Again he noticed Mitchell's hand on his arm.

Mitchell whispered, "You just wait and see, friend. Things are going to be different for you, too. From here on out."

Willy wanted to be caught up in the peace and security that seemed to surround these people. God knows, he thought, being a thief and not able to stop is a lot like being a hopeless drunk. If I could find some way to get over the craving . . . What's being poor, what's working my ass off for old man Chilworth, if I had a little self-respect and could know in my heart that I'd never be in trouble again? Why, that feeling would be the most wonderful thing in the world! To be safe. To be absolutely clean. Forever.

Willy leaned forward and put his face in his hands. He was almost swept away by an intense welling of emotion, as though Bob's speech had touched old, forgotten springs. The shell of silence and suspicion built up by the years in prison was crumbling. He felt newborn, and scared to death, and utterly naked mentally—all at once.

Bob's voice went on, and Willy shivered and shook under its sound and Mitchell kept patting his arm to comfort him.

Finally Mitchell leaned closer and spoke. "Don't worry, don't be afraid. Let yourself go. You'll be around the corner and on your way before you know it. Nothing can stop you now."

Befuddled, Willy glanced up at him. "Really?"

"Absolutely."

"How do you know?"

"Experience." Mitchell winked at him. "Just between us— I've never reminded Bob of it, and he's never remembered me. He was pretty soused that night. But I'm the guy who wanted to take him home from the mission."

Eddie had no watch, no way of keeping track of the time so he would know when to go back for Skip. He began to drive close to the curb, looking for a clock in some shop window. Finally, in a closed barbershop, he saw a clock on the back wall, made out the time by means of the light reflected from the street. It was a little past ten-fifteen.

Karen sat huddled opposite. She hadn't said a word while he was dropping Skip, while Skip was giving instructions as to when he must return. She wasn't asleep, though.

Her eyes were fixed straight ahead, as if she were watching something that kept pace with them just outside the windshield. He kept glancing her way. His impression was that she was beginning to get over the first shock of Mrs. Havermann's death, beginning to accept and believe it, and that new torments were rising in her.

Finally she said, "What will they do to us?"

"Who?"

"When they catch us." She licked her lips. "When the police catch us."

"There's something you've got to remember," Eddie said, "if you get caught and they want you to talk, and promise you things, promise they'll make it easy for you, or argue with you. It's this. Keep your mouth shut. It's the only way to stay out of trouble. If you answer just one time, correct them on one little detail they've got wrong on purpose, they'll have you tripping over your own feet before you know it."

Her eyes moved around to study him. "You mean, just say nothing at all?"

"Don't even nod your head or blink your eyes. Shut yourself up inside yourself and think about something else. Don't listen to them. Count things, remember things. Try to remember all the shoes you've ever owned, all the shoes you've worn all the way back as far as your memory goes. Or count the shows you've seen. The movies. Try to think of the titles. But don't let their words get through to you."

Her eyes were big now. "You've done that?"

He nodded. "I had to. Somebody told me about it a long

time ago, and it's the only way to beat them. Just don't listen."

She went back to staring through the windshield. Eddie was driving aimlessly. He was scared all the way through, sick over the old woman's death, and if he'd had his way would have headed out of town as fast as the jalopp would take them. But of course they had to go back for Skip. Skip was still trying to find the money.

They were in the hills above Altadena now, on a rough rutted road. Eddie looked around, seeing the sudden dropping away of lights. They had come to a section where new homes were being built. A cluster of red lanterns loomed up ahead, topping the piled earth of a new excavation. Eddie braked to a halt.

Karen roused and looked out. Some of the houses were just framework buttressed with chimneys, not roofed over. Others were almost completed. Karen said tonelessly, "Look, it's a new neighborhood."

"I've got to turn around, go back. We can't get past that ditch."

Karen was looking out now with a touch of interest. "No, let's stop here for a while. We've got to wait somewhere. Do you think there's a watchman out here?"

"I don't know. Probably not," Eddie answered, thinking of the times he and Skip had stolen things out of unfinished houses. Karen was opening the car door on her side. "Where are you going?"

She said, "I just want to get out of the car. I just want some fresh air." She stood with her head back, looking at the stars, and then moved off across the dark, rubble-dotted ground. Eddie doused the lights, got out, shut the car door. It was quite dark here now; there were crickets in the distance that only seemed to emphasize the silence around them. The red lanterns at the excavations in the distance looked like glowing coals. He could make out Karen, a dim shape under the starshine, going toward a half-finished place with a big front porch. She sat down there facing the street, put her elbows on her knees, leaned her face on her palms. She looked small and unutterably lonely.

"Why do things happen . . . the way they happen?" she asked when Eddie sat down close beside her.

"Gosh, I don't know. If I knew that, I'd be a magician." Eddie thought it over some more. "I'd be God."

The porch was brick, hadn't been swept yet, and crumbs of mortar lay on it. The interior of the house behind them gave forth a strong fragrance of sawn wood, the smells of paint and putty. He saw that Karen had cupped her eyes with her hands and was crying again.

Eddie moved closer and put an arm around her. She moved her face against his jacket. "I didn't even get to say good-by to her," she wept. "I didn't get to tell her . . . not even once . . . how I felt about living there all those years. And at the end she hated me. She hated me because I brought Skip and you to her house." She choked over her words, and Eddie stroked her hair softly. "When I first met Skip and talked to him about the money, I just thought it was a kind of joke."

Eddie was amazed at her idea. "Skip never thought money was a joke."

She cried for a while against his coat, wiping tears away with the back of her hand. Then she said, "You're different from Skip, Eddie. I'll bet you don't even know it, but you're entirely different. There's a kind of . . . gentleness about you, and Skip doesn't have it. Not a bit of it."

"Ah, Skip's okay, I guess," Eddie said uncomfortably.

"No, there's something lacking. I used to think he was tough, awfully brave, and that what was inside him was strength. But tonight I saw that wasn't it at all. Inside, Skip is—is kind of hollow. Not in a physical way. I don't quite know how to put it."

Eddie recalled something from the past. "When we were in high school I heard the principal raising hell with Skip once and he told Skip that he was immature. Something in him wasn't growing up along with the rest of him. That's all that's wrong with Skip; he just isn't all grown up yet," Eddie said.

"He's never going to grow up." She waited then as if thinking, then said suddenly, "Let's not go back for him!"

The treasonous thought was to Eddie like ice water thrown over his body. He began to protest.

"Well, we won't argue about it," she said quickly. She pulled herself closer, as if sheltering from a wind. "I don't want to argue with you. I like you. If anything separated us I'd just die."

She was awfully young and afraid—Eddie had sense enough to know this, to suspect that her clinging was based on the circumstances of the moment. But he could not help but respond to her softness, her nearness. All at once she lifted her face to his, and their lips met and clung.

She was warm and yielding. He found himself trembling. She whispered something against his face, her voice husky, almost drowsy. He spoke then, staccato, the words ripped off short with tension and urgency. "We won't go back. You're right. We'll leave Skip where he is. And to hell with him."

CHAPTER FIFTEEN

Skip stood in the shadows beside the back door for several minutes, listening. When he had first emerged from the shrubbery and stolen toward the porch it had seemed as if a sound reached him, not the sort of sound somehow that he connected with the bouncing and yapping of the dog upstairs. But now that he had waited and listened there was nothing; the house was empty and still and something in its stillness had the feeling of death about it.

Skip went into the screened porch, passing the tubs and the washing machine, on into the kitchen, then the hall. The door of Stolz's room stood open, and for a moment this startled him; but then, thinking back, he couldn't remember whether it had been closed or shut when they had fled from the house. He went into Stolz's room and pushed the door shut, not quite catching the lock. Stolz's room was his objective. Mulling things over in the diner, it had occurred to him that finding the money behind the canned dog food might have a different meaning than the one he had put on it.

Old Mrs. Havermann might have hidden the money in the kitchen *before* she'd thought of putting the new locks on Stolz's room. After the new locks were installed, she could have reclaimed the treasure from the cupboard and returned it to Stolz's room—somewhere they hadn't thought to look. Skip remembered looking under the bed, but not *in* it.

Could the money have been carefully hidden between the covers, or under the mattress, spread out thin so it made no bulge or wrinkle?

He meant to find out.

Skip went to the bed and stripped back the covers, pulled them off into a heap on the floor. Nothing. He lifted the mattress at the head of the bed. Beneath the mattress were the springs, not enclosed like box springs but the older coil type, so that Skip could see through them to the floor. There was a little dust on the floor, some rolls of cottony fuzz, and that was all. Skip dropped the mattress into place. His conviction that the money must be in Stolz's room was beginning to weaken.

He was careful about touching anything which would retain a print. He'd forgotten the rubber gloves, left them on the shelf back of the car seat along with Eddie's.

He started to take out cigarettes and matches, and then with a muttered "Oh, what the hell," went to the foot of the bed and flipped up the other end of the mattress and for a moment felt a great leaping shock of joy. There was a white-wrapped bundle there, not big; it could be a part of the money. Skip dropped the cigarette in his fingers. His hands were shaking. But then the moment he touched the wrapped object he knew it wasn't bills.

He undid the white cloth, which turned out to be a

pillow slip. Inside was a gun. It was quite small and flat with an extremely short barrel. It looked like a toy. Skip had trouble breaking the cartridge clip loose. But when he had it out, it proved to be full of neat little bullets.

For a moment he was so taken with the tiny, deadly-looking gun that he almost forgot the money. He lined up the sights, squinting at himself in Stolz's mirror across the room.

"Neat," he said, examining the weapon. "Real neat."

He put it into his pocket and then couldn't leave it there. He took it out again and kept it in his hand while he looked over the rest of the room. He found nothing, and everywhere he searched, he and Karen and Eddie had searched before.

He stood in the middle of the floor, thinking. He couldn't understand why Big Tom and his friends hadn't shown up, and then he remembered the way the house had looked, all lit up, when they had seen it across the vacant lots. To Big Tom and his friends the effect would have been the same as if the place had been on fire. Skip grinned to himself. Well, leaving the lights on had been smart . . . for a time. But now it was better to turn them out. Somebody besides Big Tom might take notice. Skip clicked off Stolz's light as he went out, circled back to the kitchen, doused the lights there, then clicked off all but one in the lower hall. He darkened the rooms where Eddie had searched and then went softly up the stairs.

He felt funny about going up here, so near the dead woman, but he wanted one more glance around. He had the gun in his hand; he liked the feel of it, the compact deadly weight of it, like a pair of brass knucks that spit fire. He passed close to Mrs. Havermann's door, and then from within the room he heard a slight noise.

The dog? Skip froze to listen. No, the dog was still down the hall, yapping and bumping around, nowhere near Mrs. Havermann's bedroom.

Mrs. Havermann . . . Hell, she wasn't dead then! She'd revived somehow. What was she doing in there?

The conviction that Mrs. Havermann had made the faint sound, like a slow-moving person shifting some article in the room, was so strong that no thought of Big Tom intruded to warn him.

I'll scare her with the gun, Skip thought. Nobody else is here now to interfere. I can beat her up a little. She ought to be plenty ready to talk by this time. He threw open the door and started inside.

Big Tom was across the room beside the open closet. He had entered the room only a minute before, had seen the woman sprawled under some fallen clothes. In that instant his mind had gulped in a vast lump of knowledge: the punks had been here; they'd bungled it; they'd run out in a panic just as he would have expected, and his own situation here in the house with a corpse was the kind of thing he dreamed about on the bad nights when he suffered from nightmares.

He ripped off his right-hand glove and bent forward to touch her, not through any instinct of mercy or a desire to revive her, but rather to convince himself that this ultimate boobery on the punks' part had actually happened, and at the same moment he heard someone come into the room behind him. His hand clawed for the gun in his belt, the big heavy gun, and then he had pulled it free and was ready to fire even as he swung around to face the room. The Luger spoke, but at this instant fiery gnats were stinging his flesh. There was no sense of impact or penetration; it all seemed to lie in his skin, a spray of needles. The bullet from the Luger entered the floor at Skip's feet. Big Tom folded forward slowly and struck the rug with his head.

Skip stood near the doorway. His expression was one of surprise, as if things had happened too quickly to be believed. The gun in his hand had seemed to act of itself. It was a very clever, quick, and willing little gun. He gazed at it and then at the big man convulsing on the floor, as if wondering at the connection between the weapon and the condition of the man.

Skip waited. Big Tom quit writhing and jerking so badly and tried to get his fingers on the fallen Luger, so Skip walked over and kicked it into the closet with the dead woman. Big Tom tried to prop himself up by means of an outspread right hand, and when the hand moved it had left a print in blood, quite distinct on the polished light-colored wood, and Skip regarded it with interest.

"You give me ideas, old man," he said. He put his own weapon in his pocket, grabbed Big Tom by the arm, pulled him nearer the closet, and then, holding Big Tom's palsied fingers outspread, he made a big beautifully distinct print on the white-painted door.

Big Tom's breathing sounded as if he were doing it through a ten-foot length of hose. "Goddamn . . . goddamn punk . . . I told Willy—"

"Shut up." Skip went to the closet and got Mrs. Havermann, brought her out and laid her beside Big Tom, and then, using Big Tom's hand as he would a paintbrush, he daubed and smeared her with his blood. "That ought to do it." He went to the door, clicked off the lights, ran down the stairs and out through the rear of the house. He was positive he hadn't left a print on any surface which might retain it. Nobody was going to raise any prints on old lady Havermann except the bloody ones of Big Tom's fingers. Skip felt like whistling.

He waited in the trees above the vacant road. The night faded toward midnight, and a sense of danger stole over him. All at once some sixth sense told him what had happened to Eddie and Karen. Skip's reaction was not one of anger. He had the only amount of loot the night had produced, some three or four thousand dollars at a guess, and he had no wish to share it with them.

He left the trees at the far end of the block and walked rapidly down to the cross-town boulevard, where he caught a bus for Uncle Willy's. He was busily packing his belongings—all of them, this time—when Willy came in.

Big Tom awoke and looked at the dark, and the phantoms fled from his brain. He knew where he was, he even knew what the thing was lying next to him, the thing whose inert pressure he felt whenever he moved. He recalled Skip at the doorway. He had not seen any gun in Skip's hand and so the source of the bullets confused him, though he had no doubt of their reality. They nested in his flesh now like fiery eggs. He was light headed, almost drained dry of blood, and he had to get out of here.

He inched and wriggled his way across the room to the door, out into the hall. Then he slithered down the stairs. The lower hall had one light burning in a bracket beside the front entry. He looked up at it and it swam, exploded into a red and purple nimbus, and blacked out. Big Tom lay on his face, thought and consciousness gone, and Mrs. Havermann's big clock, the one she had brought from France when she was twenty-seven, ticked lonesomely in the silence.

When he roused again he forced himself to his knees and reached for the front doorknob. He fell down again before he could get hold of it. He tried to figure out another way to open the door without reaching the knob, and failed. Then he remembered seeing a telephone inside the door of the parlor. He turned and crawled toward the open door across the hall.

There was enough light; he could see the phone on its little spindling table, a doily under it, lace hanging down around the rim of the table. The doily pulled off with the phone, fell on his face. It smelled of ironed starch and dust. It seemed an eternity while he fought to lift his hand, to get it away from his mouth and nose so that he could breathe again.

When he had dialed, when the phone at the other end of the wire had rung six or seven times, Harry answered. Harry sounded cross and sleepy. "Yeah? Yeah?"

"Say . . . Harry."

"Who is it?" Harry yawned. "Speak up. Say something."

"Tom. This is Tom."

"Oh." Harry seemed to withdraw slightly from the receiver. "Well, where are you? What's cooking?"

"Need . . . help."

Harry took even longer to think about this. "You calling from a public phone, huh? A bar or someplace?"

"Hav . . ." Big Tom had to stop, to catch himself against the little table. He was only half propped up; now he lay flat on the floor, the phone on the floor beside him. "Havermann house. My car's on the boulevard, near a dru . . . a drugstore." Each word involved the effort of thinking about it, forming it with his lips, summoning the breath to speak. He lost all sense of what he had said; the present word was the aim, the hope, the hurdle.

"You sound sick," Harry said. "Something happen t' you?"

"Shot."

"Man, oh man. You better get out of that house."

"Going to try." Big Tom's senses faded; fear that he would black out again, lose the phone connection, lose Harry, washed through him like an icy pulse. "Can you meet me? Drive . . . car?"

Harry wasn't willing; the silence, the waiting told Big Tom that. But finally Harry said grudgingly, "Now where did you say the car is?"

Big Tom tried to think of the name of the big boulevard. He grappled with his memory. It supplied names, other streets, other towns. Now this one— Suddenly he had it, he said it into the phone, and Harry, still unwilling, promised to meet him at the car.

No use asking Harry to come here to help him. Harry wouldn't do it. And the refusal would harden him and then he'd refuse to wait at the car. I'll make it alone, that far, Big Tom promised himself. He dragged his drained, burning body back to the front door and tried again for the knob. He passed out there, still trying.

When he became conscious again, he stared around him in amazement. This was a miracle! He was far down the sloping lawn of the Havermann grounds, almost to the curb. He had no memory of opening the front door, getting down off the porch, or inching across the turf.

Could someone—Harry? Benny?—have found him, helped him? He looked all around, but he was alone. Back across the shadowed lawns, the Havermann house looked tall and lonely. The front door stood open, the beams of the light in the bracket shone out upon the porch. The rest of the place was dark.

He felt a renewal of confidence and strength. He pulled himself to his knees, and then on hands and knees he traversed the two blocks, long vacant blocks, to the boulevard. And then it was time to rise up and to walk.

He squeezed himself over against a building, out of the light, and forced his body slowly upward. There were strangenesses: odd tremors and loosened joints and a tearing sensation all through the middle of his lungs, as if his lungs were made of tissue paper and the breath trapped in them was forcing a hole slowly wider and wider. Sweat came out all over him; he tottered off balance; a great roaring filled his ears.

"Walk, feet." Had he said it aloud? No matter. There was no one about now; the drugstore had closed. Passing, he could see inside it, the night light above the prescription counter glowing ruby red in an enormous jar of colored liquid. And then by another miracle he was at the car. He slid inside and fell across the seat.

A long while later he heard a whispering voice. It insinuated itself into his brain, rousing him from the compulsion to sleep.

"Hey! Hey! Can you sit up? Look, are there any cops around here?"

Tom listened dreamily to the voice.

"Who shot you?"

Tom said, in his mind, "The little bastard threw a handful of bullets at me—just threw them, mind you—and the damned things went all the way in, exactly as if he had used a gun. It was remarkable, very remarkable." In his dream, then, he was telling this to a screw he had known in prison, and in reply the screw, who had always been short-tempered, raised an enormous leg and kicked him between the shoulder blades and a long quivering slice of pain ran through his body from back to front. That'll teach me to pass the time of day with a goddamn screw, Tom said to himself in his mind. But then, anyway, he went on explaining: "And I didn't even see him raise his arm. What I saw, it seemed he just had his finger pointed at me and . . . zzzzzz! Like bees!"

"For God's sake, are you laughing?" cried the whispering voice.

Big Tom opened his eyes. Harry had the door open on the other side of the car, was leaning in, his face not more than six inches from Big Tom's. "I'll get you t' Doc. You remember Doc. He won't like it," Harry whispered, "but he'll do it." He grunted, pushed Tom erect, got him propped into the other corner of the seat. "Where's the key? Tom, Tom!" He was slapping Tom's face.

"Shirt . . . pocket."

Harry squeezed into the seat, poked into the pocket, got a closer look at the mess on Tom's clothes. "Jeez! My God, it's like a sieve. I've *really* got t' get you t' Doc!"

"You . . . really . . . do," Tom whispered in answer.

The motor hummed into life. Harry let in the clutch. "You had a gun? How come you didn't use it?"

"Surprise . . ."

"What about the dough?"

"I don't know. Maybe they . . . got it. Old woman's dead."

"What?" Harry's voice was a yelp.

"Dead . . . inna . . ." Too hard to say; he'd forgotten the other word. "Dead," he repeated simply.

"You plugged her?"

"Already dead."

"Who did it then? Who plugged you, for God's sake?"

"The punk." Big Tom fell over against Harry, and Harry had to fight to hold onto the wheel, to keep from crashing into a row of parked cars. "Hey, look, you're getting blood all over me! You got t' bleed like that? You got t' bleed on *my* clothes?"

Big Tom's answer was a hoarse, dragging breath which died in a sudden strangle. Harry drew the car into a side street, slowed down, studied Big Tom's bobbing face anxiously.

"You okay?"

Big Tom's mouth opened; he lifted a hand aimlessly as if to locate his lips, to see why they no longer obeyed his commands, no longer formed words, just hung loosely and fluttered with his breath. As the hand lifted, his head bowed as if to meet it. His whole body staggered forward to crash against the front of the car.

Blood began to drip heavily to the floor.

"Hey!" Harry waited a moment, looking out anxiously—this was a quiet residential street, old houses set close together in a lot of shrubs and flowers. Harry licked his lips, swallowed several times. His face was greenish in the light from the dash. "Tom?" he said softly.

The dripping was slowly decreasing and there was no answer from Big Tom, not even the sound of a breath.

Harry took out his handkerchief, carefully wiped the steering wheel, the door rim, and then used the handkerchief, wrapped around his hand, as a sort of glove while he set the brakes and doused the lights and switched off the motor. He opened the car door and slipped out and laid the handkerchief on the door handle before closing the door. Then he backed from the car a few steps and paused. He could see Big Tom in there, lying forward on the dashboard; he thought Big Tom looked exactly like a passed-out drunk and wouldn't be noticed seriously for hours, not before morning, perhaps, when it would be light enough to see the blood all over him.

"I'm sorry t' have t' do this," Harry muttered. "I just can't afford t' get messed up in it." He started away, then glanced back and whispered, "If I could help, I would. But nothing's going t' help now."

He went back to the main cross-town street and looked around. He'd taken a cab all the way out here, answering Big Tom's urgent summons, but that was before he had known what had happened. Now he wanted no one connecting him with the district, with Big Tom, or even with the city of Pasadena. He couldn't risk a cab.

He waited for a bus, and when one came he sized it up; it was quite crowded, a bunch of noisy young people in the back and the others looking tired and indifferent, not paying any attention to each other. He got on. He crouched quickly into a seat near the door before anyone could notice the blood on the side of his suit.

When he reached his flat the blond girl was in bed asleep, naked as usual, reeking with sexy cologne.

Harry sponged the suit in the bathroom, put on his pajamas, took several aspirin and a couple of sleeping pills. When he sat on the side of the bed to yawn the girl roused and grunted at him, and he said, "Shaddap!" Finally he snapped off the bedside lamp and put his head on his pillow and lay there looking at the dark.

"Just like that!" Harry whispered to himself. "What a hell of a way t' go!"

CHAPTER SIXTEEN

The long black car snaked into the drive, paused, then continued almost silently toward the house. The man behind the wheel, a huge black-haired man with a look of granite hardness about him, said, "Mr. Stolz, the front door's open."

"Yes, I see that it is," Stolz said quietly. His dark, narrow, handsome face held only a touch of dismay. He was smoking a cigarette in a gold and ivory holder; now he removed it, crushed it out in the dashboard tray, put the holder into his breast pocket. He looked closely at the house as they rolled nearer. "All dark, darker than she would have it. Someone's been here. We're late."

Marvitch nodded, guiding the car back into the shadowy area near the garage. When Marvitch had set the brakes, cut the motor and lights, Stolz got out and walked toward the back door. Marvitch caught up with him there. "This door isn't locked," Stolz said. "I know she was careful about keeping it latched after sundown."

They went in. Stolz knew the house, didn't put on a light until they had reached the hall. He went at once into his own room. He and Marvitch surveyed the mess. "She had moved it," Stolz said. "I kept it in there." He indicated the wardrobe, walked over, opened the little door that Big Tom had closed. "They made a search." Stolz looked at the up-turned end of the mattress. He shook his head. "I hate to lose the little automatic. It was quite a toy. Besides that, it might turn up somewhere later to embarrass me."

Marvitch said, "We'd better look around for the old lady and the girl. Maybe they're tied up somewhere."

"That's likely." Stolz led the way back into the hall. "Mrs. Havermann's room is upstairs. Let's look there first."

Stolz ran lightly up the carpeted steps. He kept himself lean and fit. He watched his diet, ate a lot of fruit and yo-gurt and bran crackers, and swam in the hotel pool. The desert sun kept him well tanned. Marvitch was slower, weighter. Marvitch lived on rare steaks and bourbon whis-key and eighteen-year-old brunettes. He, too, in his own way was in excellent shape. When Stolz saw what was in Mrs. Havermann's bedroom he paled yellow, and when Marvitch saw it he made a sharp indignant sound like a squeezed duck.

"Oh, my God, what a horrible thing to have happened to her," Stolz said. He sounded as if he meant it. He looked at Mrs. Havermann and then glanced away, as if the dreadful sight sickened him. "They've killed her."

"They sure have." Marvitch stared around at the room. "I wonder where the girl is?" He had never seen Karen, but Stolz's description of her had interested him.

Stolz looked quickly through the other rooms. "She doesn't seem to be here." He shook his head, as if dismiss-ing the problem of Karen from his mind. "We have to plan very carefully now."

"I don't see how we can clean this up enough to keep it away from the bulls," Marvitch said.

"Oh, we'll have to call the police. This is murder, Marvitch." He looked Marvitch in the eyes and Marvitch understood: this was a *special* kind of killing, not the sort you did and dumped in an alley or left for the buzzards out the other side of Hoover Dam, in the desert. This old lady had to be all legally accounted for, examined, and investigated. "Yes, sir," Marvitch answered. "But when, Mr. Stolz?"

Stolz's eyes were bitter. "We've got to find that damned money first."

"I should think so," Marvitch agreed.

Stolz appeared to think it over. He said, "I know the house better than you do. You don't know your way around at all."

"Money's money, Mr. Stolz. I'd recognize it anywhere."

Stolz smiled slightly.

"Not only that," Marvitch went on, "I've had things hidden from me before, and I never had much trouble finding them."

"There's no one to question, unfortunately."

"I don't mean like that. I mean cold turkey, looking for it. I had me a girl in Chicago once; I gave her a diamond brooch, and then afterwards she decided she liked another dealer better than me and she gave me the gate. I wanted the pin back. I couldn't touch her; her new friend had connections. So I hunted in her place and I—"

Stolz held up his hand. "We haven't much time."

Marvitch demanded, "You know where she had that diamond pin hidden?"

Stolz sighed. "No. Where?"

"In a box of very personal apparel, if you get what I mean."

Stolz nodded. "That was unfair, wasn't it?"

"Didn't fool me a minute."

"Go downstairs," Stolz said briskly, "and start looking. Not in my room. Everywhere else. Including the garage, the old car she kept jacked up out there."

Marvitch was glad that Mr. Stolz had allowed him to conclude his little yarn about the diamond pin. He rushed downstairs and began to turn over again the things Eddie and Skip had once tonight overturned.

Nearly an hour's work got them nothing. They concluded that the money had been taken by the thieves. Much disturbed now, uneasy and angry, Stolz called for the help of the police.

They awaited the arrival of the cops in Mrs. Havermann's parlor. The dog had been released from his prison upstairs and now lay at Stolz's feet. After obvious cogitation Marvitch said, "You know, there are some funny things about the old lady's death. She has all the marks of a strangling job. But then there's all that blood—bloody prints on the closet door, blood all the way down the hall and the stairs. There's even some over there." He pointed to the large stain in the rug by the table holding the phone. He had found the phone off the hook and on the floor when he had come searching here for the money. Off the hook, and covered with bloody prints. "I think one of *them* got shot. We ought to go out and see if there's a trail outdoors and where it leads."

"It's obvious that one of them was shot," Stolz said impatiently. "But we won't hunt for him. That's for the police. We don't dare meddle with evidence. This isn't Nevada." He was looking hard at Marvitch. "We'll be walking a tightrope here. Watch what you say, watch how you act. We just got here, and we're stunned."

They practiced looking stunned, and the dog slept until the cops came with red lights, sirens, and bright gold badges.

Skip slammed the lid of the suitcase, locked it. It was bigger than the zipper case and quite old and battered. "Well, that's that."

Uncle Willy, pale and shaken and twitchy with nervousness, sat across the room on the other bed. "Can't you tell me everything that happened? I don't want to be left in the dark. After all, I got my friends into this. Important people." Uncle Willy was thinking of Snope and of Snope's methods when he became displeased.

"You're better off not knowing," Skip said. "Just believe me, the job went sour. Big Tom goofed. Real bad. I knew when you dragged him in on it, it was a mistake."

Uncle Willy chewed a nail. "I can't understand anything going wrong for Big Tom. He's a real careful operator. Maybe you shouldn't have gone anywhere near the house tonight. Maybe if you hadn't been there, prying around—"

"Just be glad I was," Skip said. "Just be glad I was smart enough to do a little checking. If I hadn't heard those shots and seen what I had, you might be a sitting duck right now."

"No, no, I'm in the clear. Perfectly in the clear. Skip,

I don't mind telling you this job washes me up. I'm all through. I'm never going to have anything more to do with anything crooked."

"Now you're getting smart," Skip commended.

"I'm not going to ask you any more questions, either," Uncle Willy went on with an air of withdrawing from something wicked. "I've got a whole new slant on life. It doesn't have to be a rat race." His coat hung over a chair, the pockets heavy with A.A. leaflets; Uncle Willy looked over that way, his face brightening. "Yessir, I've crossed a kind of bridge and I never intend to go back the way I came."

Skip nodded, looking around to see if he had missed anything. He paid little attention to Uncle Willy's meanderings.

Uncle Willy said, "I had my eyes opened tonight. I'm not going to kick any more about working for Mr. Chilworth. I'm not going to grouch to myself and think all the time about the chances I missed and the jobs I might have pulled off, and things like that. I'm going to concentrate on myself, my own shortcomings and failures. You know, the harm I've done others, and so on. I'm going to straighten myself out. It's just a miracle, you might say, that I called A.A. and they sent me this Mr. Mitchell."

"You liked him, huh?" Skip picked up the zipper bag and went into the bathroom for his shaving stuff.

"He's the best man I ever met in my life," Uncle Willy said fervently.

"That's fine; you stick with him," Skip advised.

Uncle Willy's gaze followed Skip as he moved around the room. "There's no money coming at all?" he ventured timidly.

Skip glanced over at him. "You'd better forget you ever heard of any money."

"And you didn't . . . uh . . . get a chance to—"

"From outside?" Skip demanded scornfully. "With them plugging away at each other in there like a shooting gallery?"

"I just can't understand it." Uncle Willy rubbed a hand around over his thin head of hair. "To think Big Tom and those men he knew would have a blowup like that."

"They did, and that's why I have to clear out. If the girl talks I'm cooked. If they find her, that is."

"She's not waiting somewhere for you?" Uncle Willy demanded, having forgotten his decision not to ask any more questions. "I thought she had your jalopp, maybe, was outside in the street, or maybe running an errand."

"Eddie has the jalopp," Skip said. "If he brings it back here, push it in the garage, will you? If he doesn't, it's okay." Privately Skip thought: He took the bitch off my hands, he's welcome to the heap. He had the two bags stuffed with his clothes and belongings now, the zipper bag and the old battered case. Skip went over to the door. "Well, so long, Unc. I'll be seeing you. Remember, if the bulls give any sign of thinking you were in on this thing tonight, you know from nothing."

"I was at the A.A. meeting," Uncle Willy said, the new light beginning to shine again in his weary eyes.

In Union Station, Skip went into the men's room, entered a cubicle and shut the door, and then, standing spraddle-legged above the bags, he unbuttoned his shirt and took out the two packs of bills and counted them. One pack had twenty hundred-dollar bills and the other had twenty-five. He was the possessor of forty-five hundred dollars in crisp legitimate currency. He extracted two of the bills, put the rest back inside his shirt, unlatched the door, picked up the bags, and returned to the main lobby.

His real desire was to get to Las Vegas and try to run the money into an important sum with luck; but Las Vegas was Stolz's territory and it was just possible the money might be recognized over there in some manner. Not probable, Skip thought, but possible to the degree that he felt nervous over it. The next best, though much farther away, was Reno.

He bought a ticket to Portland, Oregon. This would take him through Sacramento, where he would get off the train and buy another ticket east.

In case anyone wished to trace him there would be a little difficulty. He wasn't thinking now of the police, but of Stolz. He had no desire ever to meet again the big man with the granite face and the granite fists. People like that were, in Skip's opinion, just plain undesirable citizens.

Eddie parked the car in the alley, some two or three doors from home. Karen whispered, "Will you be long, Eddie? Will it take much time?"

"I've got to pack a few things, not much."

Her face floated in the dark, pale as a flower, and Eddie could make out the endearing curve of lip and cheek, the fringe of lashes, the soft gleam of her eyes. Already Karen's face had taken on the familiar aspect of the well-beloved. It seemed to Eddie that he had known her forever. He leaned into the car to kiss her once again. She put up her hands to frame his face, to pull his mouth to hers. When the kiss ended she whispered, "You're just wonderful, Eddie. You really are!"

Eddie felt wonderful. He had the sensation of having found a small, exclusive, and rather unbelievable treasure much more to be prized than the mundane one of money. Karen belonged to him. He belonged to her. It had happened on the front porch of a house being built in an unknown part of Altadena. No matter who eventually bought and owned that house, a little bit of it would always be his and Karen's.

He went quickly down the dark unlit alley to the slatternly back fence, found the gate, went in past the heaps of unboxed refuse and wine bottles, to the back door of the house. He let himself in. The smell left by his mother's cooking, the chili, the masa and grease, the coffee, was rank in the kitchen. He stole through to the main room, crossed it softly in the dark, and tapped on the bedroom door.

He heard the bedsprings creak, some sort of muffled drunken jabber from his father, his mother saying, "Go back to sleep. I'll see to it." The door opened and there she stood, dimly visible in the vast white cotton gown. "Eddie?"

"Come out and close the door."

She obeyed. She came into the room, shut the door without rattling the catch, then went to a table and switched on a lamp there. She looked over the lamp at Eddie, and he saw the worry, the anxious dread in her eyes. "Something's happened?" she whispered.

"I have to go away tonight. Right away."

She pulled the edge of the gown up over the lump at the base of her throat. She stood by the lamp for another moment, then sat down slowly. Her face crumpled; she hid it in her hands. She was crying.

"Don't worry about me," Eddie said. "All I need is a few dollars. You do have something hidden away, don't you, Mama?"

She nodded without lifting her head from her hands. The enormous goiter bulged from between her wrists like the head of a baby under the skin there, a baby which had worked its way up there trying to be born. She trembled, her flesh quivered, but the big lump under her skin was firm and quiet as though it were not a part of her. "Can you tell me?" she whispered.

"I'd better not. Then you won't know; they can't threaten you."

"I wouldn't tell anyone anything," she said through her shaking hands.

"No, Mama."

"Is it . . . really bad?"

"Yes, it's bad. It's as bad as it can get."

She lifted her eyes, her mouth still covered, perhaps to conceal its trembling. Her eyes were already reddening. "Somebody killed?"

Eddie looked away, not answering. His mother picked up the sleeve of the gown between her fingers and rubbed her eyes on the cotton. "I had a feeling. A long time I've had a feeling. I kept saying to myself, No, it's just the class Eddie's interested in. He's going to get a job, make honest money. All those troubles are behind him, the bad company he kept and all that talk about how to live easy without working."

Eddie walked around the room a little. He knew his mother had the right to say what she was saying. She had stood by him in every scrape he'd been in, from the earliest time when he'd still been in grammar school and had been caught stealing money from the teacher's purse. He and Skip. He hadn't told anyone that Skip had been in it with him. He'd kept his mouth shut; the principal had whipped him with a wooden paddle, had warned his mother that a second offense would mean the juvenile court. And she had taken the principal's harsh words with dignity, with composure, and, going home, she had stopped on a street corner and shyly, softly, she had asked Eddie if he would like a chocolate soda at the drugstore fountain. Eddie couldn't remember a time when this Mexican mother of his had not had love and patience and gentleness in her, and so now he listened to her grieving and kept his mouth shut and waited.

"I will say a prayer first, and then I will get you the money," she said. "Kneel down, my son."

He knelt down, feeling a little awkward, and she began saying the Our Father in Spanish. After that she prayed to the Blessed Virgin, asking the help of the Mother of Christ for her son, asking that this most pure and merciful Mother who had known terror and despair in her time on earth should now listen to the anguish of another for her child.

When the prayer was finished she rose, crossing herself,

and went into the kitchen. She brought a broken-backed chair from beside the door and placed it in front of a cupboard. She said to Eddie, "On the top shelf. The red can, the tomatoes. Take what is in there."

Eddie got the can down, opened it.

"There is fifty-six dollars," his mother told him. "Not much. It will take you a little way. Write to me when you get where you are going. Not here, send it to Mrs. Valdez. She'll give it to me at church."

Eddie stuffed the money into his pants pocket. They exchanged a last embrace. His mother's body was big and flabby inside the gown; her hair smelled of oil; she had a faint odor of wine, too, from being around his father, from being shut up in the bedclothes with a stinking drunk.

"I'll write to Mrs. Valdez," Eddie promised.

"Go with God," said his mother in farewell.

CHAPTER SEVENTEEN

They drove up the coast. The night had turned chill and patches of fog swept in from the sea, obscuring the highway. Eddie began to yawn, to have difficulty keeping his eyes open. Above Santa Monica they came to an oceanside park and campground. It was full of trailers and tents, but Eddie pulled in anyway, crowding the jalopy in among some squatty evergreens. Karen got out. She was shivering. She had no wrap of any sort. Eddie stripped the blanket off the seat, the old Army blanket Skip had used to cover the holes in the original upholstery. He spread it on the needles, leaves, and trash under the trees and then he and Karen lay down and rolled themselves up in it. Down here next to the earth, sheltered from the seawind, they were fairly warm. During the night Eddie was awakened by Karen's crying. When he touched her hair softly it was damp with tears.

At about eight o'clock the clatter of the other campers awakened them. Eddie unwrapped himself from the blanket, helped Karen to her feet. Karen staggered, gained her balance, looked around. It was a dark, overcast morning, quite foggy and cold. She rubbed her bare arms with her hands, licked her lips. There was a grainy exhaustion and heat behind her eyes. Her mouth tasted sour and soiled. She thought suddenly of the big Havermann house, its quiet and its security, clean hot water and towels, food waiting to be cooked, and a sense of loss and desolation shook her. For the first time she seemed to see, in a material way, what Mrs. Havermann had given her.

She walked over to the car, not wanting Eddie to see her tears, and waited while he replaced the blanket on the torn upholstery. She noticed that Eddie had an air of confidence, of knowing what he was about, even of meeting a challenge, and this comforted her a little.

They kept headed north. When they got close to Oxnard Eddie said, "We've got to eat. We need every dime we've got with us, though. I'm going to try something."

I need a comb and a towel, Karen said to herself. I never knew you could feel so dirty, just sleeping out one night by the roadside. I feel as if I could soak for a week. She closed her eyes; the thought of food didn't interest her.

Eddie passed up several rather nice-looking cafés after studying them briefly. Finally he swung in beside a somewhat shabbier café, small, sitting by itself a little distance from the highway. There was a graveled lot growing up with weeds. The signs all needed repainting. On the roof of the café a metal vent had fallen over and lay at the rim of the rain gutter. Eddie cut the motor, set the brake, got out of the car. "Wait here," he said. He bunched his jacket over his chest against the chill air, went to the door of the café and entered.

The only person inside was a woman of about sixty. She wore a clean cotton housedress and a blue calico apron, a blue cap over her thin gray hair. She had coffee going in an old-fashioned pot, grease on a griddle, bowls set out with little boxes of cereal in them. Eddie spraddled a stool. "Cup of coffee," he said.

She looked out the window at the car, then back at Eddie. "Cold this morning, ain't it?"

"It sure is."

"Along the coast here, some days you'd never know what time of year it is. Just always foggy and cloudy and cold. Yessir." She poured coffee into a thick mug and put it down for Eddie.

Eddie said, "I'd like breakfast, a real breakfast, but I'm too broke to buy it."

"Well, that's too bad." Her tone didn't betray any interest or sympathy. She started to turn away, then looked back. "Who's that out in the car?"

"My wife," Eddie said.

"If she's cold and wants a cup of coffee, I'll give her one," the old lady said. "Free."

"Well . . . I do appreciate it." Eddie stood up. "What we need is pancakes and bacon and eggs. I sure wouldn't mind working for it if you'd let me. I could do dishes."

"Dishes are done," she snapped back. Then, as if relenting a little, "Say, you are kind of husky. How are you with a pick and shovel?"

Inwardly Eddie instantly shied off; he hadn't had any intention of involving himself in anything more laborious than an hour or so of pearl diving. But under the old lady's alert, somewhat cynical glance he found himself saying, "Well, maybe I'm no expert, but I'm willing."

She put both knuckly hands on the counter. "I'll tell you what happened. My husband—he and I run this place —he's been digging a ditch for the new septic tank out back. County said we had to have one, gave us sixty days to do it. Well, he's been digging every day for a week and yesterday he ain't feeling so good and today he can't hardly move a muscle. He's almost seventy. Shouldn't a done it at all, of course."

She was watching Eddie closely. Her mouth was pursed up now, her expression one of penny-pinching miserliness. "If you're hungry, you and your wife—well, there's a job for you."

Eddie put a dime on the counter and shook his head. "That would be a kind of big job in trade for a meal. Thanks anyway."

"Now, wait a minute." She swallowed a couple of times as if the next words were coming hard. "I ain't said just trade for a meal. We need the ditch dug. We got to get it dug, somehow. Them damned plumbers want four dollars a hour." By an instantly regretful expression, Eddie knew she wished she hadn't parted with this bit of information. She stumbled around then and finally said, "How's this— I'll pay a dollar an hour. Two days if it takes that long."

Eddie reached for the cup, downed the last of the coffee. "I'm sorry. It's not enough."

"Meals throwed in. You and your wife."

They stared at each other measuringly. She was the kind of little old woman, Eddie thought, that if she'd been left on a farm all her life wouldn't have known the time of day, but being exposed to the sharpers and chiselers among the touring public, was as sharp as a pin. "A dollar and a half an hour, I might think it over."

She came back instantly, "Dollar'n' a quarter. That's my top limit."

"Meals too? All we want?"

She peered out the window, probably trying to size up the girl in the car, wondering how much she'd eat. Eddie was big and, exposed to the labor of ditch-digging, could be expected to be ravenous. The little old lady gulped down some thrifty objections, nodded her head, and said, "It's a bargain."

Eddie hurried back to the car, opened the door on Karen's side. "I've made a deal. We eat here. Order whatever you want."

She brushed back her hair and looked at him in a dazed, indifferent manner. Eddie, knowing how she must feel, urged her out of the car. "You'll feel a lot better when you eat. You'll be surprised at what some hot coffee will do."

A lot of anxiety went out of the old lady's expression when she saw how small and slender Karen was. She drew a cup of coffee quickly, put it on the counter, took Eddie's cup and refilled it. "Now," she said, "Ham and? Toast?"

"Pancakes," Eddie said. "Plenty of butter and syrup." He took off the jacket and laid it on a stool and saw the little old lady sizing up his muscular arms. He thought, We need a name. He remembered the name of a classmate in metal class, Arnold Dykes. He said, "I'm Arnold Dykes and this is my wife Kay." Kay for Karen. Karen glanced at him as if she hadn't quite caught what he had said.

The little old lady shifted the pancake turner to her left hand, offered her right to the girl. "I'm Mrs. Mosby. You can call me Ellie if you've a mind. Kay's a pretty name. You're a right pretty girl, too."

She seemed taken by Karen. Perhaps something in the girl's hunted, exhausted look touched her. When the food was put before her, Karen ate it indifferently, almost mechanically; but Eddie noted that her color was better almost at once, that some of the dazed look went out of her eyes.

They were finishing a third cup of coffee when a couple of trucks pulled in next to the place and four truck drivers entered. They were big men, hungry as horses; Mrs. Mosby scurried around, chattering with them, and Eddie saw they were regulars, the kind she depended on to keep the café in business. He was surprised, then, when Karen got up and took all their dishes out to the kitchen, found a rag behind the counter, wiped up.

He caught her wrist across the counter. "Hey," he said in a low tone, "you don't have to do that."

"I'd rather, than just sit." She went back to the kitchen and came back with a blue apron tied around her middle. The truckers were showing signs of interest, and Mrs. Mosby was openly pleased.

"It wasn't in the deal," Eddie said stubbornly, standing up from the stool. Karen looked at him tiredly.

"I'll make my own deal, then." Suddenly tears stood in

her eyes; her expression seemed weak and sick. "Oh, Eddie, let's don't quarrel. Things are too bad to add that along with the other. Let's just be friendly."

He shrugged. Mrs. Mosby was pleased, and Karen perhaps would have something to take her mind off their predicament. When Mrs. Mosby had served the truckers she led Eddie out behind the café. The restrooms were here at the back, and the sewer lines from them and from the kitchen drains lay exposed in the hard brown earth. She indicated where Eddie was to dig, and how deep.

"Over there." She was pointing now to a small house, half hidden in a clump of young pepper trees. "That's our place. My husband's in there now, him and his lame back. He'll be watching you, but don't let it bother you. He won't get out to try to run things." By a certain vindictive tone in her words Eddie judged that she was somewhat put out with her ailing husband.

The morning passed slowly. Eddie took a coffee break about eleven. In the café a couple of Japanese truckers, their load of lettuce outside, were finishing coffee and doughnuts. Karen was washing up in the kitchen. Old Mrs. Mosby was as chipper and cheerful as a sparrow.

Why not? Eddie thought uncomfortably. Hell, the two of us working—she's got us over a barrel. Or thinks she has. A sudden strong dislike for the old lady came over him.

Close to noon, she took off across lots for the house in the pepper trees, and as soon as she was out of sight Eddie put down the shovel and went into the café. Karen was alone there, polishing the griddle. Eddie went to the cash register, pushed the no-sale button, and inspected the amount of money in the till. About ten dollars, he thought, mostly in quarters, half dollars, and dimes. He slammed the drawer.

"Now, what did you do that for?" Karen demanded, staring at him.

"For nothing."

"She's a nice old lady," Karen said.

"I didn't say she wasn't."

"You don't like it because I'm helping her, do you?"

"I don't care." Eddie was conscious mainly of boredom. The job in the back yard meant nothing to him. He stared out of the window at Skip's jalopp, the shabby little car, and wished he'd never stopped. At the same time he knew that what he was doing now his mother would call honest work, and she would never understand his dissatisfaction and lack of interest. In order to have understood her son his mother would have had to follow him through his whole life, first as a half-Mexican in a mixed school, belonging to neither faction, and then as a friend of Skip and being molded by Skip's opinions and desires.

Skip got off the bus in Reno, checked his suitcases in the station, and went out at once to look the town over. He had never been in Reno, though he knew it was different in some ways from Las Vegas. There was no Strip, for one thing, no long arm of luxury hotels and casinos stretching toward sucker-land in California. Reno lay close to the High Sierras, the Donner Pass country, and it seemed at once more of a frontier town and at the same time more compact and sophisticated, like a city. Once inside the gambling clubs, however, the resemblance to Las Vegas was startling. Here were the same vast ranks of slots, the identical green tables, craps, roulette, twenty-one, the same clang of coins and, for Skip, even the same faces, the expressionless know-nothing masks of players and club employees alike.

Skip turned in one of the hundred-dollar bills at the cashier's cage, getting tens in exchange. He went to a crap table, watched the action for a couple of minutes, then tossed three of the tens across to the dealer, who stacked thirty silver dollars in front of him. Skip put five dollars on the line. There were about a dozen men at the table. The shooter was an old fellow with the withered, weather-worn look of a desert rat. On his first shot he threw a seven and Skip's money was increased by five. Skip let it ride, added ten. Again the old fellow threw a five and a two. Skip withdrew his winnings on some psychic impulse, fortu-nately, for the old fellow crapped out on his next throw.

Skip went to the next table. When he finished there he was more than five hundred dollars to the good. Feeling hungry and thirsty, he headed for the café at the rear of the club.

In the cashier's cage the assistant manager was counting and examining the money taken in and took a second and longer look at Skip's hundred-dollar bill. He nodded to the girl cashier. "Wait a minute. Something I want to check." He took the bill with him, went to a door set flush on the wall, touched a button, and waited. In a moment he was admitted to an inner office, a steel-lined room built like a vault.

He took an FBI flyer from a desk drawer and began to study numerals on it and compare them with the numbers on the bill.

In the café Skip had just been served a New York-cut steak, Caesar salad, whipped Idaho potatoes, fresh green peas, and coffee royal. He ate dreamily, looking at the Gold Rush murals painted around the walls.

Eddie said, "Look, it's nearly five. I'm going to knock off."

Mrs. Mosby was drawing him a cup of coffee. "Sure, that's all right. You've done fine. Got a lot more digging done than I thought you would." She glanced at him anxiously as she put the coffee down in front of him on the counter, perhaps sensing his mood of disgust and boredom. "Tell you what, I'll close up about seven, you and your wife can have the place to yourselves. There's a cot stowed in the rafters, up above those shelves in the storeroom. It ain't much, just a double cot and a pad. I'll get you some bedding. What I thought, it'll save you the price of a room."

Karen was stacking dishes under the counter. "That's nice of you, Ellie." She hadn't looked up. She'd been acting funny, in Eddie's opinion, ever since the middle of the afternoon. Scared, more than ever. Dry-mouthed with fright, eyes big, hands quivering.

He noted a paper down the counter, pulled it toward him. It was an L.A. paper, and as soon as he saw the headlines he knew what was eating Karen.

RICH WIDOW SLAIN IN PASADENA
TEEN-AGER, WOMAN'S WARD, MISSING

Eddie glanced at Mrs. Mosby, saw she had turned away and wasn't paying any attention, and began reading the news article avidly. The information was scant but bewildering. The last Eddie had seen of old Mrs. Havermann she'd been in the door of the closet, stiffening, cooling, showing signs of strangulation but otherwise not marked up. Here in the paper it stated she had been found in a blood-smeared room, evidence of a savage gunfight all around her, and the cause of death was undecided.

Eddie felt as if his head whirled. *What was this?*

He licked his lips and read on. Stolz had told the police he had arrived at the Havermann house at around eleven-thirty, answering a phone call from Mrs. Havermann to Las Vegas. Mrs. Havermann's message, delivered to him at the hotel, had said that she was nervous over the possible presence of burglars. According to the paper, the police were quite curious as to why the elderly woman had appealed for protection to an ex-son-in-law as far away as Las Vegas, but Stolz stuck to his tale that Mrs. Havermann had lived almost alone and had grown eccentric. He had also informed the police of the disappearance of the young girl whom Mrs. Havermann had raised from the age of nine or ten. There then followed a good description of Karen.

There were photographs on an inner page: the Havermann house from outside, Stolz—coming out the front door with his hat up as if accidentally shielding his face—and a picture of Karen with braids at about the age of twelve. It still looked a lot like her, Eddie noted uneasily.

In a framed box was a detailed description of the girl,

with an appeal from the police for anyone seeing her to get in touch with them.

The general belief seemed to be that Karen had been kidnaped by the robbers who had invaded the house, had had a gunfight, and had decamped.

Stolz said that nothing seemed to be missing.

Not a word about the money, Eddie thought. He put the paper down, tried to figure out what had happened. Stolz had his money safe, that was sure. He was keeping quiet about it, too. Then another hunch struck Eddie with dreadful impact.

Skip had been shot in that room. Stolz had killed him and hidden his body, dumped it somewhere. Or else Skip was wounded and was hiding somewhere and perhaps dying slowly.

A terrific sense of treasonous guilt shot through Eddie. His course was plain to him. He would have to go back to L.A. and find Skip.

CHAPTER EIGHTEEN

Mrs. Mosby locked the front door of the café and clicked off all the lights in the dining area. She showed Eddie where the cot was, stuck up high in the rafters, the pad tied in a roll beside it; and while he was getting the cot down, setting it up and unrolling the pad, she went to her house and brought back two pillows in fresh cases, a couple of sheets and a blanket.

When she had gone again, when the bed was made, Eddie flopped on it and stretched himself with a sigh. "I'm beat. Chrissakes, I'm beat to the socks," he said. Then he looked around for Karen. She had disappeared into the kitchen. "Hey, what are you doing?"

"I've got to scrub and wash my hair," Karen called back.

Eddie lay and listened to the wet splashy noises from the sink, and then he drowsed. He hadn't worked so hard since the last time he'd been in honor camp, repairing the roads in a county park. He woke when Karen sat down beside him. She'd found an old broken comb, was using it to straighten her hair. She smelled fresh and clean. He lifted himself and pulled her close, loving the clean smell and the softness. Then he had to talk about what he'd read in the paper.

"I've been trying to figure it out. Stolz must have caught Skip and shot him, but Skip somehow got away. He'll need help; my God, he might be bleeding to death somewhere this minute."

A bleak frightened look settled in her eyes. "Don't talk about him. Don't think about him. Forget him."

"I can't do it." Eddie spoke in resignation, bitterly.

"We have each other," she said desperately. "We don't need him."

"I shouldn't have run away, ditched him like that. It wasn't any kind of a thing to do."

"No, it was the right thing to do." She lay down close to Eddie and tucked her head against his chin, and he saw the fluff of her hair against the dying twilight.

He pulled up her face, kissed her, forgot the tiredness and began to stroke the soft line of her back beneath the slip she'd kept on as a nightdress. Then the discomfort of his own guilt intruded. "I've got to go back and see what's happened to him."

She pulled away, rose on an elbow. "What? What did you say?"

"I've got to go back." Eddie's brown eyes, so brown they seemed black, were thoughtful in his dark, square face. "It's this way. Skip and I—well, we were always a team. Always together! We never let each other down."

"I'll bet he's let you down plenty of times," Karen said in sudden anger. "I'll bet he's tricked you and left you out on a limb over and over again."

Eddie sat up; he felt irritated and insulted. Still, he couldn't blame Karen for being upset; she was young and inexperienced. He controlled the rush of angry words. "This is what I planned, why I planned it. Now look. We were going to sleep here tonight, weren't we?" Karen nodded; he went on: "So if I slip out and drive back to L.A. during the night, get back here by daylight, who's going to know about it, and what difference will it make?"

Karen had moved away to sit crouched at the foot of the bed. Inside the rayon slip she looked slim as a child, frail, defeated. Her skin glowed with a white shine under the dim light from the window high in the storeroom wall. "Please don't go. Oh, please, Eddie! Stay here with me. Or if you want, tomorrow we can go on somewhere else."

The tone was so desperate, so pleading, that Eddie almost relented.

As if sensing that he was on the verge of giving in, Karen rushed on: "If you go anywhere near that house, the police will grab you. I'll bet they'd grab you if you drove by a block away and even looked over at it."

"I wouldn't go out to *your* place," Eddie said. "What I'd better do, the first thing to do, is check with Skip's uncle."

"You can do that over the telephone!"

"I don't know the number."

"Well, you know Skip's name!" Her voice grew higher, shriller, with every word she spoke.

"It's not in Skip's name, or his uncle's name. His uncle works for a man—I've heard Skip mention the man's name but I can't remember it. I wouldn't want to put in a long-distance call anyway, asking about Skip. You know, if the cops are wise, the phone could be bugged, or the uncle even taken in on suspicion—oh, hell, anything could have happened!"

She flung herself at him, clutched him, squeezed so tight that Eddie was astonished at her frantic strength. "Don't go! Don't go!"

Eddie loosened her grip patiently. "Now of course Skip's uncle doesn't know anything about the Havermann job," he went on, thinking aloud. "So he won't know, unless Skip got to him, that Skip needs help. That's what I've got to do, get to him and explain that Skip's in trouble, must be shot up and ought to be found and taken to a doctor."

She threw back her head, brushed at her hair, looked directly into his eyes. "I know it isn't Skip who's hurt. He's too smart, too clever and quick. If anyone is shot, it's somebody else."

"It has to be Skip," Eddie explained. "Stolz is okay. The paper said so."

At the last Karen offered Eddie the one gift she thought would keep him, and he accepted it instantly and delightedly, loving her passionately for the offering of it; but when it was done he got up from the bed and put on his clothes and went out, instructing her to lock the door after him.

Thinking to cut some distance from the trip, he took the Ventura Boulevard route for San Fernando Valley, planning to enter L.A. through North Hollywood and Cahuenga Pass; and in an isolated part of the west valley, surrounded by walnut groves and areas of rocky hills, everything but what the headlights showed blanketed in moonless dark, the old car burned out a bearing, the engine exploded with

a grinding breakage, and he was stranded. He was nowhere near L.A., had no idea what the next town might be
or where it was. Karen and Mrs. Mosby's café might as well
have been a thousand miles from him. All he could do was
to wait in the car until daylight.

When Mrs. Mosby came over from her own place at about
seven, Karen was already up and dressed, had the cot
folded and stacked in a corner, the pad rolled and tied, the
borrowed bedding placed neatly on top. She was in the dining room, stacking dishes. Coffee water was boiling.

Mrs. Mosby exclaimed with pleasure and surprise. There
wasn't a lazy bone in the girl's body. She was young and
pretty, the truckers would be attracted. Mrs. Mosby made
plans to keep them here—and then noticed the absence of
Eddie. "Now where'd he take himself off to?" She peered
out through the front windows. "Car gone, too, huh?"

"He went over to see a friend," Karen said stumblingly.
"Last night. He . . . didn't come back."

Mrs. Mosby studied Karen, saw that tears were just under the surface and that the girl was terribly frightened
and upset. Had a fight, she concluded from her own experience, remembering the long ago years when she had been
a bride, easily hurt and dismayed. "Well, we'll just go ahead
and have breakfast, and he'll show up. You scold him good
when he comes. Make him eat crow. Ain't every young fellow has as pretty a wife as you."

They ate. The food was hearty and filling. Mrs. Mosby
emptied her change bag into the cash register, unlocked
the front door, and the place was open for business.

Karen worked as if afraid to stop. She scrubbed up all the out-of-the-way spots, stacked canned goods in the storeroom, tidied the soaps and brushes beneath the sink. She seemed determined to keep her hands occupied, to keep thought, introspection, and self-concern at bay.

At about eleven-thirty Mrs. Mosby went back home to attend to her husband's wants. During this time Karen was alone in the café. A trucker came in with an L.A. morning paper. He left it when he finished eating. Karen read it in panic. Her description was boxed on the front page now, in large black type. Mrs. Havermann's death had been attributed to heart failure brought on by asphyxiation. Murder. A man identified as the intruder in her home had been found dead of gunshot wounds in a car some distance from the Havermann house. Reading this, Karen had an almost unbearable surge of relief, thinking Skip was dead and Eddie would know it and come back—but the paper's account continued, to say that the dead man had been identified as a middle-aged ex-convict named Thomas Ranigan, commonly known among his criminal associates as Big Tom.

His fingerprints matched the bloody ones found in the dead woman's room and on her person. The police were now trying to trace Ranigan's movements on the night of the murder and to account for the accomplices who must have quarreled with him and shot him.

Karen felt almost dizzied by this crazy story which seemed to have no connection with the facts as she knew them. Eddie had made a frightening mistake in going back. Probably he was in the hands of the police right now. As the paper dropped from her fingers, the black-boxed description of herself seemed to boom almost audibly from the page: *seventeen years old, five feet three to four, slender build, dark brown hair, blue eyes, attractive appearance.* It never occurred to Karen that the items listed in the box could apply to thousands of other young girls. She felt picked out, spotlighted. She felt as if a million eyes, a million pointing fingers, searched out her shrinking body. She was convinced that the next customer to walk into Mrs. Mosby's café would recognize her instantly.

The place was empty temporarily. It was chance, perhaps her only one. She ran to the cash register, punched a key, removed a handful of bills, half dollars, quarters. She rushed around the counter and out the front door. Beyond the parking lot the highway hummed with traffic.

She walked, turning whenever she heard a car coming, trying not to look guilty and scared, trying to look like an ordinary girl out for a walk, needing a ride. She was in the outskirts of Oxnard now, among orange-packing plants, lots selling farming equipment, truck lots.

The big tanker began slowing some distance behind her. By the time Karen looked around, she could see that it was going to stop. The big tires spun gravel off into the roadside ditch, the brakes whooshed with a sound like a giant sigh. Then from the cab the driver was leaning across to look down at her. He had a heavy face, black eyebrows, signs of a beard beneath his skin. "Hey, kiddo. You going someplace? Want a ride?"

She nodded swiftly. "Yes, I want a ride. Please."

"Where you headed?" He smiled now, the lips drew back from his teeth, his heavy chin widened.

"Where are you going?"

"Don't care, huh?" He put an elbow on the rim of the cab window. "I'm headed for Salinas; from Salinas I'm taking a load north. Eureka. Know where that is?" He smiled, waited; but Karen was struck dumb, and he added, watching her curiously, "Three hundred miles north of San Francisco."

She said from a dry mouth, "That's fine."

She took a step toward the cab door and he put his hand down inside as if about to touch the door latch there. Then he sized her up a little more closely. Perhaps something young and inexperienced about her warned him off. His look clouded and he said, "Well, now, wait a minute." After a pause he added, "That's a hell of a long trip. Sure you want to go so far?"

He was stalling, she saw. She looked up at him. The heavy, sweating face was like a mask hung in the sky above her, denying her, shutting her away from escape.

She tried to think of some way to convince him he should take her, to force some hint of invitation and knowingness into her eyes so that he might be attracted to her, but she was too inexpert and too unsophisticated to bring it off. She could not summon any coaxing remarks. She looked up at him mutely.

"You really got to go?" he asked softly.

She nodded.

His hand dropped to the door latch, and the wide door swung out and for a moment she saw the wide padded leather seat and his thick legs and his booted foot on the brake pedal. "Get in," he said.

She took a single step on the gravelly shoulder of the road, and then wordlessly she turned and, running, almost falling, she went headlong back the way she had come.

Skip awoke and looked around the hotel room. He felt good, in spite of the long hours at the crap tables the night before, plus the drinking he had done after midnight in order to stay awake. He rolled over, took the phone off the cradle, asked the desk for the time. It was a quarter past ten. Skip asked to be transferred to room service, requested a shot of Scotch, coffee, and tomato juice sent up at once.

He crawled out of bed, inspected the roll in his pants pocket. He had over seven hundred in tens, twenties, and fifties. The remainder of the money he'd found in the Havermann house was still intact. After some thought he took an envelope and paper from the writing desk across the room, wrapped the Havermann money into the writing sheet and sealed it in the envelope, wrote his name across the envelope; and when the boy came with the whiskey, coffee, and juice, Skip tipped him two dollars and asked that he turn the envelope over to the desk with instructions to lock it in the safe.

Skip then lay in bed and enjoyed his breakfast.

He made plans for the day. Blackjack first. He used to be pretty good at it. An old con in the road camp had showed him a trick or two. But while Skip was dressing he became displeased with his clothes. Hell, they were rags. He postponed the gambling until he had bought a new suit, shirt, shoes, and tie. Then he hit the blackjack tables, three clubs one after the other, and by ten minutes to two he was broke. He went back to the hotel and requested his envelope from the safe.

He thought that the clerk handed it over with a glance of cynical amusement, knowing what was inside, thinking of the sucker being peeled of his money, and inwardly Skip cursed and raged.

He went back to Virginia Street and by chance, recognizing the façade, re-entered the club at which he had begun gambling the evening before. He gave the girl a hundred-dollar bill and she seemed to delay changing it, fussing with money in the cash drawer below the counter; and then, distinctly, perhaps because some sixth sense was tuned for an alarm, Skip heard a buzzer sound somewhere in the rear of the club, near the entrance to the café.

He put his face close to the grill. "Something wrong with my dough, sister?"

She met his gaze calmly. "No, sir. I've had to call for some small bills. The manager will be here in a minute."

Skip looked around. A tall man dressed in a tux, white shirt, black tie was coming toward him through the ranks of slots. He had his eyes fixed on Skip in a way which Skip recognized. He was memorizing Skip's face. Skip reached at once inside the cage, snatched his bill back, and turned for the door. "Just a minute," called the manager in a voice of authority.

Skip walked rapidly, bumping into people, shoving others flat against the machines as he passed. One old woman screeched at him, "You better watch it, buddy!"

There was a cop on the sidewalk, twirling his club; Skip went right past, not looking up, the bill clutched tightly out of sight in his palm. He heard voices behind him, looked back briefly. The manager was talking to the cop, his arm raised to point Skip out.

Skip opened his hand and took one incredulous look at the bright new bill. What in hell was wrong with it? There were no visible defects. If it had been counterfeit the girl cashier, long trained to detect phonies, would have spotted it last night. He glanced behind him, found the cop making purposeful progress in his direction. Skip darted into an alley.

It was not an ordinary alley. It was paved and walled with tile, bursting with neon light even by day, the entrances of several gambling clubs open, patrons idling there in the doorways. Skip started to run.

The cop shouted behind him. Skip darted into a club, worked his way across it, found himself at a dead end. There was no other exit on this side.

A sliding door clicked open and he saw the inside of an elevator. He rushed into it. The operator looked at him politely and said, "Sorry, sir, we're going down. Basement offices." His look invited Skip to leave before he was suspected of being a holdup artist.

Skip ran for the front of the club, out upon the sidewalk, across Virginia Street, down the block, around the corner beside a bank. Here was a cross street, not as crowded, no gambling clubs but cafés and small stores. He went into a souvenir store and pretended interest in some painted ties; and then in another two minutes the cop was out there, staring in at him.

There wasn't anything else to do. Skip grabbed for the

little gun in his pants pocket, the tiny toy he had inherited from Stolz. The little gun spoke quickly and willingly, and a spray of little holes danced across the plate glass at the front of the store. The cop ducked. Something big and black sprang into his hand. The sound it made was nothing like the small *pockety-pock* of Skip's tiny automatic. It went *booomp*.

Skip went down, clutching the rack of ties.

He had three bullets in his liver, one in his groin, and by the time he reached the hospital in the city ambulance he had only moments to live. A nurse bent over him, asking his name, his home address, and Skip spoke to her in return.

The doctor came toward the stretcher with a hypo in his hand. "What did he tell you?" he asked of the nurse.

"I can't repeat it," she said. "It was too nasty."

The doctor reached for Skip's arm, then suddenly for his pulse. But Skip was dead.

CHAPTER NINETEEN

Eddie woke at about daybreak. He was chilled, his muscles stiffened by the long hours in the seat of the car. He had spent a lot of time in thought; and the conclusion, though he hated to face it, was that he did not have money enough to repair the jalopp, even if the old car had been worth it.

He hitched a ride eastward with a chicken farmer who had a pickup with crates of white leghorn fryers in the back. The old man chewed snuff and talked about raising pullets and the price of chicken feed and how much he got for chicken manure and feathers. Eddie learned for the first time, though he didn't think about it long, that chicken feathers were used for fertilizer.

At a roadside garage Eddie got out, while the chicken farmer waited for him, and rang the night bell. The mechanic stuck his head out of a window at the back. "Yeah?" Eddie went back there to talk to him. He described what had happened to the car, its age and condition, and the mechanic shook his head. "Tell you what, after I've finished breakfast I'll run out there and take a look at it. Won't cost you nothing," he added, perhaps because Eddie showed so few signs of having a bankroll. "Where you headed now?"

"L.A."

"Stop here on your way back to the car and I'll tell you what I think, what it'll cost to fix it, and if I think you might as well junk the heap, or what."

"Thanks a lot."

The chicken farmer let him out in Reseda, and on the far outskirts of the town Eddie caught a second lift, this time from an expensively dressed heavy man driving a Cadillac. The man had whiskey on his breath and proceeded to unload his troubles on Eddie. He had spent the night with his girl friend, and his wife was going to raise hell. She was getting ready to take the kids and leave, and he was scared to death she wouldn't even be home when he got there. His father-in-law was threatening to run him down with a shotgun. At the same time he couldn't leave this other woman alone. She was his former secretary, married to an airline pilot who was gone a lot. She had red hair and weighed one hundred and fifteen pounds and had been a New York model.

Eddie was glad to escape in Studio City.

He caught a bus, using some of the money his mother had given him. It was getting later by now, the sun was high, and he began to worry about Karen. She'd think he wasn't coming back. He should have telephoned from Reseda.

In downtown L.A. he tried to call the Mosby café in Oxnard, but the operator could find no number listed for it.

Eddie recalled distinctly the big black phone on the wall at one end of the counter and told the operator about it, and she suggested that it may have been a pay phone and told him that such phones were not listed under the name of the establishment; there was a separate list for them and it would take a little time to check this. Eddie told her he couldn't wait and hung up.

By means of several bus transfers he finally reached Uncle Willy's home. He went up the stairs softly, rapped at the door. Uncle Willy didn't answer; but presently, from up there, Eddie saw him come out of the rear door of the big house at the front of the lot and throw some bread crumbs on the lawn for the birds.

Eddie went down there. Uncle Willy noticed him and stood by the back door, waiting.

"Is Skip around?"

"Skip?" Uncle Willy looked innocent and wily, his old face with its startling foxy resemblance to Skip turned up to the sky as if expecting something to fly by within his field of vision. "Skip who?"

"Your nephew." Eddie had never met the uncle before, but the family pattern was too marked to be mistaken. "I'm Eddie. You know."

"You're Eddie?" A touch of vindictive dislike appeared for a moment on Uncle Willy's features, to be smoothed away at once as if by magic. "Oh yes. Eddie. Been a friend of Skip's for a long time, haven't you? You boys have been in trouble together, lots of trouble." Uncle Willy came down the steps and faced Eddie closely. "Let me tell you just one thing. It's time to change. It's time for you to change and for

Skip to change, to remake your lives, to give up the things that are going to ruin all the years ahead."

This was not the sort of talk Eddie would have expected, since he knew from Skip of his uncle's record.

"Now, Skip has gone," Uncle Willy went on. "He was here packing his bag when I got home from the A.A. meeting and I talked to him, as much as he'd let me, and then he left. I'm not sure how much of an impression I made. Maybe I didn't put it right. Maybe I should have waited until he was ready to listen. But now you're here, and my conscience wouldn't let me rest unless I'd told you a few facts for your own good." He looked earnestly and determinedly into Eddie's reluctant eyes. "The life you and Skip have led is nothing but a blind alley. It'll get you nowhere."

Eddie said, "Where is Skip, please? I wanted to make sure he was all right, not hurt, not shot up or anything."

"He's fine, perfectly fine," Uncle Willy said. "It was Big Tom was shot up. Skip sneaked over there, wasn't supposed to, of course, and heard it going on. Big Tom must of made a terrible booboo somehow. You just be thankful, Eddie my boy, that Skip eased you out of that job when he did. It could have been *you* on the receiving end of those bullets." With a final, emphatic nod Uncle Willy went into the rear porch and shut the door.

Eddie rapped on the door, full of anxious questions, but Uncle Willy called from the kitchen, advising him to go away and behave himself. Finally Eddie left the place, went down the block to an intersection, bought a paper off a newsstand, and read the account of the finding of Big Tom, dead in his car, and the identification of Big Tom as the intruder at the Havermann house. There was no mention whatever of Skip, nor of himself or Karen.

Eddie couldn't figure out this puzzle, but some things were obvious. Skip hadn't been injured. He had been packing to leave when his uncle had reached home. He had apparently heard some sort of shooting inside the house where the dead woman lay. Could it have been possible that some other outfit had planned to get Stolz's dough on the same night that they had?

Much confused, as well as relieved about Skip, Eddie set about the long chore of returning to Oxnard.

Anxious over the long delay in returning to Karen, he decided not to stop and see about the mechanic's report on the jalopp. He had a hunch what the mechanic had to say, anyhow. Something about throwing good money after bad —if he was honest, and he'd looked honest. Eddie bought a ticket on a Greyhound bus and rode straight through. At Mrs. Mosby's café he found the elderly woman working at a counter full of customers, Karen nowhere in sight. Mrs. Mosby jumped on him for leaving Karen so long, and between scurryings told him Karen was feeling poorly. She was in bed, on the cot in the storeroom.

When Eddie entered the storeroom, closing the door behind him, he could see Karen lying there on her back, face to the ceiling, eyes big and quiet, almost dreamy. She looked thinner, fine-downed. Mrs. Mosby had tacked some cotton material over the window, dimming the light, but Karen glanced over and saw Eddie at once. She said weakly, "I can't really believe it's you. I was sure the police had caught you."

He sat down, put his arms under her, lifted her close. "Not a chance. It's all over now."

"It's just beginning," she whispered against his face.

"*We're* just beginning," he agreed.

"No, I don't mean that. What I mean is, we're going back. I thought of calling the police here, but it might make trouble for Mrs. Mosby. And she's been kind. We'll have to go back to L.A. and get hold of a policeman there."

Eddie put her down slowly. His expression was one of stunned amazement. "You don't mean it."

"Yes, I do. As soon as I get over this chill, or whatever it is, I'm going to dress and leave." She was looking up into his eyes with a steady, earnest gaze. "Don't you see, what we were talking about in connection with Skip, that he wasn't grown up, that there was something in him that would never develop; well, that would apply to us, too, if we didn't go back and clear our consciences."

Eddie pounded his shirt. "I don't have a conscience! Chrissakes, a conscience to make you put your head in a noose, I wouldn't want a thing like that!"

"Yes, you do. And I do. We're grown up now, Eddie. We can take what's coming to us. Perhaps it won't be too bad. Perhaps, a long time from now, we can see each other again." She moved closer, twined her hand in his. She gazed at him in a wholly new way, Eddie saw, calm and unafraid and utterly loving. A convulsion seized Eddie; he thought he was going to be sick. The thought of the cops, the questionings, the ordeal of being charged and condemned and put away ran through his mind like a leaping fire.

"You must have a fever," he said to her. "You're out of your head. Crazy."

"No, I'm not. I've just got over being sort of crazy, I guess. I thought I could run away, leave everything. Leave everything I'd done, what I'd been. When you didn't come back I panicked; I tried to hitch a ride on the highway. And then I saw"—her voice sharpened—"I saw what my whole life would be from then on. Just running. And not really getting away at all."

He argued with her. But nothing moved her or changed her. And finally, in some way Eddie couldn't comprehend, some of her assurance and the peaceful acceptance transferred themselves to him. He didn't try to fool himself about the actual situation. It was going to be tough; God, was it going to be tough! But since they'd be turning themselves in, confessing, perhaps there would be something to look forward to a long time from now. With everything wiped clean, paid up, no need to run and hide.

He lay down close to her, and she stroked his hair and murmured to him. It seemed then to Eddie that the years he had known with Skip, along with Skip's values and Skip's outlook on life, dropped completely away so that for the first time he was really himself.

Eddie's mother had spent a wretched, sleepless, and tearful night. In the early dawn she arose, taking care not to wake her snoring husband, and went out to the kitchen. In the back of a cupboard, hidden from sight, was a box in which she had stored some mementos of Eddie's growing up—school cards and various items of correspondence garnered through the years. Some she'd kept to reassure herself, good grades, encouraging notes from teachers. Other bits she'd retained to worry and puzzle over.

During the night she had decided, in view of the circumstances, to burn all of this material. In some way, in the future, something in it might be damaging to her son.

She took the box to the sink, brought matches from the stove, and then began to burn the cards and notes, one by one.

A handwritten letter which had worried her particularly, coming as it had from an official in the California Youth Authority, someone who had taken an interest in Eddie, caught her eye just as she set a match to it. The words were distinct on the white page.

> . . . *your son, I feel, is in danger of becoming a type of person called, in modern parlance, a socio-path. In other words, someone without moral sense in whom all ethical feelings are stunted. A man without compassion or conscience . . .*

The flame crept upward. She felt the heat in her fingers. She dropped the sheet into the sink, and it became crackling ash.

"Not my Eddie," she said, looking down at the blackened, curling remains. "I know better."

The page gave a final pop. She turned to the next item in the box.

On the morning of the third day the patrolman on guard at the rear of the Havermann house took notice at last of the anxious dog. He went to the rear door of the house and rapped, and Stolz interrupted his breakfast in the kitchen to answer. "This dog's hungry or something," said the cop. He was a young husky cop with alert eyes and a square, businesslike chin. "You got anything to feed him?"

"I've been feeding him well," Stolz answered, regarding the dog with indifference. "He's just restless, I suppose, since his mistress is dead." Stolz wore crimson pajamas and a light silk dressing gown, oriental straw mules. He hadn't been up long. He was eating scrambled eggs with yogurt and stone-ground whole-wheat toast. He had made Marvitch hunt up a healthfood store. In the store Marvitch had tried to become acquainted with the eighteen-year-old brunette clerk. "Perhaps you'd better tie him out beside his doghouse," Stolz offered. "Then he won't be in anyone's way."

The cop took the patient, anxious collie out to his doghouse beyond the garage, squatted inside the heavy blue uniform, reached for the chain attached to the side of the opening. Then he got lower on his haunches, actually put one neat blue knee on the dirt, and peered hard inside. "Well, I'll be switched," the patrolman said to the dog. "No wonder you were worried. There isn't enough room in there for your fleas." He wooled the dog's head with his hand, and the big collie jumped around, overjoyed at this show of friendliness. "What is all this stuff?"

The cop reached inside and pulled out a plastic pillowcase, zippered shut, which through its pink color seemed marked faintly green and white. The cop unzipped the opening and stared in upon what he had found.

He tried to say something, but his tongue froze.

It was money, an unbelievable amount of cold green cash, and finding it like this, outside a bank or similar reservoir, had the funny effect of making it look like a lot of printed paper. He jiggled it, and other packets came to view, all fresh hundred-dollar bills packed into pads of similar size.

He shoved off the bouncing dog, got to his feet, and with the plastic case swinging from his fingers he went through the kitchen to the phone in the front of the house, passing Stolz at the table on his way.

Stolz got quickly to his feet, went into his room, and dressed in nothing flat. Marvitch had returned to Las Vegas; there was no way he could reach him at the moment. Marvitch would simply have to look after himself.

Stolz was on his way out the front door when the dog met him, bouncing and barking, tremendously happy that these human beings had arranged at last a place for him to sleep. Stolz aimed a kick at the collie; at the next instant some instinct warned him to look behind him.

The cop was there, the money in one hand and an authoritative gun in the other. "You'll please wait, sir. Inside."

Stolz went back inside. He braced himself. He was sharp and fit and clear-headed, healthy as an ox, and it was surprising that a shock like this could make him feel so disorientated and dizzy.

He said to the officer, "I had nothing to do with the kidnaping, nothing at all; even the FBI will understand that.

I just bought a piece of the loot." He shrugged and the motion almost sent him off balance, as if he were drunk.

"It's a hell of a lot of dough," the cop said.

Stolz looked at it shimmering with newness inside the plastic case. "Ruin and death," he said, blurting it out with melodramatic suddenness. "Ruin and death."

He put his hands over his face and began to weep.

Biographical Note

Notes

BIOGRAPHICAL NOTE

Born Julia Clara Catherine Dolores Robbins on December 25, 1907, in San Antonio, Texas. Daughter of W. H. Robbins and Myrtle Statham, who married in Caldwell County, Texas, in 1901. Father died and mother remarried to a Mr. Norton. Moved with mother to Kern County, California, by 1920. Mother divorced and married a third time, to Oscar Carl "Arthur" Birk, in 1922. Took stepfather's surname; family moved to Long Beach, California, by 1930. Published poems while completing graduate studies at the University of California; enrolled in a nursing school. She worked as a nurse at Hollywood Hospital, and later became a teacher before pursuing a professional writing career. In 1934 married Beverley Olsen, a radio operator on a merchant vessel whom she later divorced. Married Hubert Allen "Bert" Hitchens, a railroad investigating officer, who had a son, Gordon (later founder of *Film Comment* and contributor to *Variety*). Together they had a son, Michael, and a daughter, Patricia. As D. B. Olsen, published two novels featuring Lt. Stephen Mayhew, *The Clue in the Clay* (1938) and *Death Cuts a Silhouette* (1939); twelve novels featuring elderly amateur sleuth Rachel Murdock: *The Cat Saw Murder* (1939), *The Alarm of the Black Cat* (1942), *Catspaw for Murder* (1943), *The Cat Wears a Noose* (1944), *Cats Don't Smile* (1945), *Cats Don't Need Coffins* (1946), *Cats Have Tall Shadows* (1948), *The Cat Wears a Mask* (1949), *Death Wears Cat's Eyes* (1950), *Cat and Capricorn* (1951), *The Cat Walk* (1953), and *Death Walks on Cat Feet* (1956); and six novels featuring Professor A. Pennyfeather: *Shroud for the Bride* (1945), *Gallows for the Groom* (1947), *Devious Design* (1948), *Something About Midnight* (1950), *Love Me in Death* (1951), and *Enrollment Cancelled* (1952). Published play *A Cookie for Henry* (1941) as Dolores Birk Hitchens; novel *Shivering Bough* (1942) as Noel Burke; and novels *Blue Geranium* (1944) and *The Unloved* (1965) as Dolan Birkley. Co-wrote five railroad detective novels with Bert Hitchens: *F.O.B. Murder* (1955), *One-Way Ticket* (1956), *End of Line* (1957), *The Man Who Followed Women* (1959), and *The Grudge* (1963). As Dolores Hitchens, published two private detective novels featuring California private eye Jim Sader: *Sleep With Strangers* (1955) and *Sleep With Slander* (1960); as well as stand-alone suspense novels *Stairway to an Empty Room* (1951), *Nets to Catch the Wind* (1952), *Terror Lurks in Darkness* (1953), *Beat Back the Tide* (1954), *Fools' Gold* (1958), *The Watcher* (1959, adapted for the television series *Thriller* in 1960), *Footsteps in the Night* (1961), *The Abductor* (1962), *The Bank with the Bamboo Door* (1965), *The Man Who Cried All the Way Home* (1966), *Postscript to Nightmare* (1967), *A Collection of Strangers* (1969), *The Baxter Letters* (1971), and *In a House Unknown* (1973). Jean-Luc Godard adapted *Fools' Gold* into the 1964 film *Band of Outsiders*. Died on August 1, 1973, in Orange County, California.

NOTES

In the notes below, the reference numbers denote page and line of this volume. No note is made for material included in standard desk-reference books.

16.14–15 You ain't got . . . that swing."] From "It Don't Mean a Thing (If It Ain't Got That Swing)," a 1931 jazz standard by Duke Ellington (1899–1974) and Irving Mills (1894–1985).

16.20 Sousa] American composer John Philip Sousa (1854–1932), whose marches included "The Liberty Bell" (1893) and "The Stars and Stripes Forever" (1897).

35.8 jalopp] Jalopy, a dilapidated old car.

42.24–26 the Sands, the Sahara, the Flamingo, Desert Inn, the Dunes, Thunderbird] Las Vegas hotels: the Sands operated 1952–96; the Sahara opened in 1952 and closed in 2011, before reopening in 2014 as SLS Hotel & Casino; the Flamingo opened in 1946 and is currently operated by Caesars Entertainment; the Desert Inn opened in 1950 and closed in 2000; the Dunes opened in 1955 and closed in 1993, and after its demolition the Bellagio was built in its place; the Thunderbird opened in 1948, changed its name to the Silverbird in 1977 and El Rancho Casino in 1982, and closed in 1992.

110.8 Packard] The Packard Motor Car Company of Detroit, Michigan, which began operations in 1899 and went out of business in 1958, the year of *Fools' Gold*'s publication.

211.27   Donner Pass] Mountain pass near Truckee, California; it is named for the party of westward emigrants who in 1846 were snowed in and suffered starvation and heavy loss of life, some allegedly resorting to cannibalism.

This book is set in 12 point Wessex, conceived by Matthew Butterick and finished at Boston's Font Bureau in 1993. The typeface was inspired by the "surprising beauty" of the wide-bodied italic complement of Caledonia, the now-ubiquitous book font created in 1938 by William A. Dwiggins, the typographer who designed 329 books in three decades for Alfred A. Knopf and who is perhaps most famous for coining the term "graphic designer." The sans-serif display type is Lichtspielhaus, an ultra-condensed version of Lichtspiele, created by Stefan Huebsch of Typocalypse, a typographic collective in southwest Germany. The slim letters emulate the credits on movie posters and evoke "a time where neon lights and marquee letters decorated cinema facades."

The paper is acid-free Glatfelter Offset; it exceeds the requirements for permanence established by the American National Standards Institute.

Text design by Donna G. Brown.

Composition by Dianna Logan, Clearmont, MO.